I WON'T PLAY A FOOL FOR YOU

Christian & Ivy

NIKKI BROWN

Chapter One

CHISTIAN

"Ohhhhh mmmyyyy God! Yesssssss, Christian, that feels so good!" she cried out as I moved slowly in and out of her.

"Damn girl," was all I could say.

"You make my body feel so good."

"Shut up and take this dick," I told her.

I was tired of hearing her mouth. I just wanted to get my nut and get home before Ivy started with her bullshit.

I know what y'all thinking, what the fuck was my problem? That Ivy was gonna shoot my dumb ass, and you're probably right. I don't know what the fuck was wrong with me, I've been fucked up ever since I heard that shit about that abortion. I knew I said that I would forgive her but that shit was easier said than done. Even with the baby that she was carrying now, I still couldn't get over the fact that she killed my seed and didn't tell me. In my mind, it was like if she could do something like that, what else was she capable of? She could say sorry a million times and it still wouldn't help how I feel.

I lost all trust in her and our relationship. I started second guessing myself and shit, thinking that maybe she was right, maybe I wasn't fit to be a dad with the life I lived or some shit.

After a while, I just stopped giving a fuck. I started doing shit that I normally wouldn't do. Don't get me wrong, I love Ivy, I just hate what she had done.

I told myself that I would never cheat, but that seemed to be the only thing that helped me to get that shit off my mind.

I started fucking with Keri a couple of weeks ago. I told myself that it would just be one time so I could get this shit out of my system, but I've been tapping her almost every day since the day I met her.

Keri was a cool ass chick that worked in the credit union. She was cute and the sex was okay, but more than anything, she was cool to talk to. Keri had a husband and just as much to lose as I did, so I'm sure that my secret was safe with her.

When I first noticed her, it was right after Ivy told me that she killed my baby and hadn't told me, so my mind was fucked up. Keri stepped to me first and I turned her down because I was determined to make it work with Ivy. Then, right after we got back from Barbados for Messiah and Reign's wedding, shit went all bad.

She kept questioning me about what Messiah and I were

talking about on the plane and why my phone kept going off and shit. I know that shit had to be her hormones, but she was taking shit too far. I wasn't the one that couldn't be trusted—it was her.

We had a huge fight, and I stormed out and headed to handle some business that landed me at the bank. Keri tried her hand again, and on that day she succeeded, because she clocked out and we headed to the hotel.

I wore her ass out and we had been meeting up every day after her shift.

"Oh shit! I'm 'bout to cum, baby," she moaned.

There she goes with that 'baby' shit.

"Fuck, I'm nutting," I said as I filled up the condom.

I pulled out and headed to the bathroom of the hotel that we always stayed in, so that I could flush the condom. The one thing that I would never do was get caught up with getting another bitch pregnant.

"Why do you always do that?" Keri asked.

"Why wouldn't I?"

"I'm just saying, you act like I'ma try and trap you, hell, I got shit to lose too," she said with more attitude than I was willing to deal with.

"Yo, I hear what you saying, but I gotta make sure shit is good on the home front, so the extra precautions are very necessary."

"If shit was so good on the home front, you wouldn't be here fucking me," she said, pissing me the fuck off.

There was one thing that I always told her and we had

agreed on, and that was to not bring our home life into this. We were just fucking and we both understood that. I talked to her about a lot of things that were going on with me and Ivy, and she told me about her husband too. But, we always said that we would never say anything negative about the other person's business, but here she was doing just that.

I walked towards her with my eyes locked on hers. She already knew that I was pissed. Even though we had only been fucking around for a couple of weeks, she had picked up on some of my mannerisms.

I backed her into a wall and looked down at her little short ass. Unlike Ivy, she was on the slim side, and although she was cute, I would take some meat any day. She had nothing on my baby, which again made me question why the hell I was doing what I was doing.

"Don't say shit about my wife," I gritted.

"She ain't ya wife, remember?" she smirked.

I wrapped my hands around her throat.

She didn't know the real Christian; all she knew was what I wanted her to know. She didn't know that I could have her ass missing quicker than she could get her next sentence out. The only reason I would allow her to breathe was because technically, I was in the wrong for telling that bitch my business. She should never have known shit about my relationship. That was my fuck up.

"Don't ever talk about my wife again," I said, tightening my grip. "Bitch, you don't know what I'm capable of."

Her eyes got big, so she knew I wasn't bullshitting.

At that moment, I realized that I needed to stay the fuck away from her. If she was getting me to the point where I was putting my hands on her, I needed to wrap this shit up and do right by my baby.

"Aye, you know what? This shit was fun, but yo' ass getting too comfortable, so we just gon' end this shit right now."

"I think you' re right," she barely got out because I had yet to let go of her neck.

I nodded my head; that shit was easier than I thought it would be.

I let her go and she dropped to the ground, holding her neck. She looked up at me with the cutest mug. I couldn't help but let out a chuckle. That didn't help the situation because she jumped up and started to get her things together to leave.

"Look Keri, I don't want any hard feelings. Aight?"

I needed to make sure that she wasn't going to be one of those chicks that like to start shit because I cut things off.

"Fuck you, Christian," was all she said before she walked out of the door, slamming it behind her.

Right when the door slammed, my phone went off.

I looked down and it was Messiah.

"What up, bruh?"

"You tell that nigga I'ma fuck him up, got Jess questioning me and shit," Shamaad yelled in the background. "You know my paranoid ass almost shot her white ass for trying to ask me where I been. Get yo' shit together nigga, got me having to explain myself and I ain't did shit."

Shamaad actually sounded frustrated.

"Tell that nigga to shut the fuck up," I laughed, picturing him pulling his damn gun out on Jess. I swear I felt sorry for her.

"Man, what up, bruh?"

"Don't fucking 'what up, bruh' me. What the fuck I tell you about lying on my ass? I don't want nothing to do with the shit you got going on in your house," he fussed.

Fuck, I had used him as my alibi and forgot to tell him again. My ass was really losing it.

"Yo' shit is starting to spill into my household, and you know I ain't having that shit. You need to get that shit together and I mean now."

"I know, bruh, I ended that shit tonight," I tried to reason.

"Nigga, you been saying that shit since you fucking met that bird. You mean to tell me she is more important than Ivy and yo' seed, nigga?"

Here he goes, always fucking preaching like his ass was perfect. I wonder if Reign know his ass was trying to open up a got damn strip club? I bet she didn't. He needed to worry about that instead of worrying about what the fuck I'm doing. If anything, he was supposed to have my back.

"Nigga, you are supposed to have my back!"

"What the fuck does yo' dumb ass think I'm doing, Chris? I'm trying to make sure that you don't lose the best thing that's ever happened to you," he said, getting loud.

Messiah was a chill nigga until he got pissed, then all hell broke loose.

"She fucked up, man, yeah I agree. But got damn, man the fuck up. Get over that shit before you watch another nigga sit around with your woman and raise your kid."

"You already know that shit ain't happening."

"Muthafucka, you keep being stupid and you ain't gon' have a fucking choice!" Messiah yelled into the phone right before he hung up.

I sat there thinking about what he said and he was right. I needed to stop the childish shit and get myself together. I just didn't know how. I didn't know how to look at her and not see her laying on that table getting my baby sucked out of her. I dream about that shit, and the more I thought about it, the more it bothers me. I needed to find a way to get over this shit because the minute she thought she was going to be with someone else was the minute I would go on a killing spree.

"I knew his ass was lying, talking about he had business. If you hadn't been there, I would have never known."

I was livid. I had called Reign to see if she had seen Christian because he had been pulling disappearing acts since we had gotten back from Barbados.

"Girl, calm down. Maybe he was going to do business and got sidetracked or something."

I know good and damn well this bitch wasn't trying to reason with me on this shit. I had half the mind to cuss her out, but I needed her right now, and I knew that if I pissed her off, she would hang up on me.

"Got sidetracked into some pussy, that's what the fuck he did," I all but yelled. "I know that nigga, he's been acting funny ever since we had that fight. If he knew he couldn't forgive me for that shit, he should have told me and we both could have went our separate ways."

I know that getting the abortion and not telling him was wrong and I take full responsibility for that, but I thought that I was doing what was best for me at the time. I was in no way shape or form trying to hurt him. I was looking out for our future. I really didn't think that was what we needed at the time.

We sat down and talked about all of this before we even went to the Barbados for Messiah and Reign's wedding. He was fine then, talking all good and shit. He had given me false hope about our future and everything that we were going to accomplish. Here we are though, me calling my best friend trying to see if he was there or not.

"Girl, chill out; you are just hormonal. When he gets home, I'm sure he will have a good excuse as to why he wasn't where he said he would be."

"Well, I guess we will see because the bastard just pulled up."

"Ivy, do not—"

I didn't even let her finish because I knew she was about to tell me not to act a fool, but she should already know what was about to go down. I don't know why she stays trying to preach and shit. She just told me that she was going to burn down the strip club that Messiah was building that he thought that she didn't know about, but she was telling me to chill.

I looked down and my phone was going off and it was Jess.

I'm positive Reign had called her, but I didn't have time for that so I rejected the call.

I tried to calm myself down so that I could have a calm and effective conversation, but I thought about the way he had been acting, how he looked me in my face and lied just a few hours ago. The more I thought about it, the more pissed I became.

When he walked in the house, I wanted to slap that fucked up look off of his face. He looked like he had done some shit. He couldn't even look me in the face, he just walked straight to the room. If he thought his bitch ass was about to shower, he had another thing coming.

"Where you been, Christian?"

I asked it in a way that let him know that I already knew what it was. He just needed to tell me the truth because if he lied and I had to find out on my own, then there was going to be hell for him and anybody involved.

"Man, Ivy, please don't start this shit! I'm tired and I just want to shower and lay down. We gotta get up early in the morning for the doctor's."

He reached out to touch my stomach and I slapped his hands down.

"Don't fucking do that, Ivy."

"No, fuck you, Christian. I'ma ask you one more time," I put my hands on my hips and stood directly in front of him, belly poking out and all. "Where the fuck was you?"

"I had some shit to take care of," was all he said.

"With who?"

"What's up with all of the questions, Ivy?"

"Because something in the got damn milk ain't clean."

"What the fuck does that even mean?"

His facial expression was confused mixed with aggravation.

"It means some shit ain't adding up, nigga, and yo' ass been lying."

"You don't have a fucking right to question me with that bullshit you did," he said and my heart sank to my stomach.

I knew that the abortion was the reason he had been acting the way he had, but I refused to let him use that as an excuse to treat me bad.

"We talked about that, I told you that I was sorry."

"Well, I guess I'm sorry too."

I tilted my head to the side and took a good look at him, because if he was about to tell me what the fuck I thought he was and actually thought that shit was gonna be okay, he's about to get a rude awakening.

I walked closer to him and he stood there, still not making eye contact with me.

"Sorry for what, Christian?"

"Man, nothing. Can I go shower?"

"Why the fuck you gotta come home and go to the shower?"

"Why the fuck not, Ivy? What the fuck?"

He was getting frustrated but I didn't give a damn.

"What are you sorry for? You fucking around?"

"Man, I don't have time for this shit."

"Answer the question!"

He was really starting to piss me off.

"Which fucking one? You have asked me about 69 questions since I walked in the got damn door."

I covered my face with my hands and let the waterworks begin. I hated what we had become. I loved Christian, but we didn't have to be together to raise this baby. I would walk the fuck away before I stick around for some bullshit, fuck that.

"The most important one, muthafucka, are you fucking around on me?"

Guilt covered his handsome face. His body language already told me what I needed to know, but I still needed to hear him say it.

I don't know why I needed it to come out of his mouth, but I did.

"You buggin'."

"Nah, you stalling. Spill it."

"I'm not doing this with you, Ivy. Yo' ass is pregnant and hormonal."

"No, nigga, yo' ass is a liar and a cheater," I said, mimicking his tone and facial expressions.

"You always wanna fucking fight, you want something to fight about, huh?"

His ass was yelling and pacing now. He should know good and well that shit does not bother me at all. I will shoot his big ass and think nothing else about it.

"You need to calm the fuck down and answer the fucking question before you find yourself single as fuck," I matched his tone.

"Maybe that's what the fuck I want, Ivy; you ever think about that shit?"

Everything just stopped in that moment. I didn't even have a response for what he just said. As bad as I wanted to cry, I just couldn't give him the satisfaction of knowing that what he had just said crushed my soul. I couldn't even argue with that. The only thing that I wanted to do was get the fuck away from him.

I took a few steps backwards to put space in between us.

He reached out to grab me, but I snatched away. The last thing that I needed was for him to touch me, and I damn sure wasn't trying to hear his sorry ass apologies because I knew it was coming. That is all he seemed to do lately, fuck up and apologize.

"Baby, I didn't mean that shit," he started but I put my hands up to stop him.

I hated when people got mad and let all of their true feelings out, and then when they realize what they've done they want to apologize.

"You know I didn't mean that shit, Ivy. I love you, you know that."

I just shook my head and grabbed my favorite blanket off the bed. I wobbled to the spare room in the house and slammed and locked the door.

I was kicking myself for not keeping my got damn house.

After everything happened, that was one of the things he made me promise to do—get rid of my house. Now look.

KERI

I didn't know who Christian thought he was dismissing me the way he had dismissed me. I have been what he needed me to be since he finally gave in to my advances. Yes, I'm married, but my husband was just so boring. Christian brought the spark back in my life, even if it was just for a short time.

I met Christian at the bank where I worked. I had been throwing myself at him for months and he would never bite. One day, he had walked in and he looked pissed. I asked him what was wrong and he told me to mind my fucking business. At that point, I decided that I had to have him, so I turned up the heat and just asked him to fuck me. I must have caught him at the right time because he told me to meet him at the hotel around the corner from my job. I looked forward to our daily meetings, but now I didn't know if I would still have that.

I pulled up to my driveway and noticed that Jerimiah was home. I laid my head back on the headrest because I was not in the mood to deal with his shit tonight. I missed the way we used to be when he wasn't so worried about appearances and the case he had to work on.

Jerimiah and I were high school sweethearts and had been together since. We used to be so in love when we were broke, but when the money started to roll in, so did the problems. There were no more dates, or nights where we would just chill and laugh for no reason at all.

I guess that was what I was looking for with Christian, but he told me numerous times that there would never be anything with us, except sex. He even threatened to kill me if Ivy ever found out. For some reason, that shit turned me on.

I finally mustered up the energy to go into the house and face the music of the warden. I could hear him now talking about why I decided to wear my hair in its natural state, instead of straight like he liked it. I didn't feel like being ridiculed after the fight that I just had with Christian; I just wanted to go to bed and remember the way he handled my body.

I walked into the house and surprised was an understatement. There were candles everywhere, and rose petals lined the foyer, continuing down the hall that led to the kitchen. I followed the petals and I could have passed out where I was standing.

"What's all this?" That was the only thing that I could think to say.

"I just wanted to do something nice for my wife."

I could tell something was up by the way he said 'wife'. He lingered on the word a little longer than I thought that he should have.

I looked into his eyes and for a second and thought I saw what I had been missing all these years, but with one blink, he was back to being the cynical asshole I had grown accustomed to.

He grabbed my briefcase out of my hand and put in on the floor, then held my hands so that I could step out of my Giuseppe pumps. He even went as far as to lean down and kiss me. He put some tongue action in it and if I didn't know any better, I would think that he was trying to get some tonight.

"Go ahead upstairs, shower, and I laid something on the bed for you to put on after."

What the hell was going on? I didn't trust this and it was starting to scare me. That was a shame. I couldn't even be comfortable with my husband doing something nice for me.

I went upstairs to do what he asked because if I didn't that would start an unnecessary fight; I didn't have time for it. Christian had already fucked up my night, so I didn't need anything else to go wrong.

I walked into the bathroom and turned on the shower water to wash away all of today's events. I hated the way Christian had just dismissed my feelings in this whole situation. Yes, I knew that he was in a relationship, but from the sounds of it, things were coming to an end. He told me from the beginning that this was a short-term thing and he warned me not to get addicted. How could I not though? Christian was tall, handsome, beautiful eyes, and had a sex game that would drive a damn nun crazy. Too bad he belonged to someone else.

"You okay up there?" I heard Jerimiah yell up the stairs.

"Yeah, I'm fine. I will be down in a minute."

"Great, I have a surprise for you."

"I can't wait," was all that I could think to say.

The last time he told me he had a surprise for me, I walked around with a black eye for two weeks because of something I put on Facebook. One of his colleagues had seen it. The bad part about all of it is the only thing that I posted was a meme that read, *Treat her like a QUEEN and she will make you her KING.*

I didn't think anything was wrong with it, but clearly he did, and I found out just how much when he walked in the door that night.

Jerimiah used to be the most caring and loving man that I had ever met. It wasn't until he started working for my father that he turned into the monster that he was now.

My dad was a controlling bastard and I don't know how my mom had stuck around this long with his pompous ass. He ruined a perfect man, because Jerimiah was nothing like he used to be.

I finished getting dressed in the lingerie he had purchased

for me, and I said a quick prayer that this night would end on a positive note.

I walked down stairs and there he was standing there with two flutes filled with champagne. My husband was a handsome man. He was the complexion of sweet caramel, tall, muscular, and one of the most intelligent men that I knew. It's a shame that he turned into the monster that was standing before me.

"You are so beautiful," he said, smiling at me.

"Thank you."

I gave him a faint smile.

"Come sit down."

The look on his face seemed sincere, but the look in his eyes screamed evil and I've always heard the eyes never lie.

I walked into the kitchen where he was standing. I took the glass that he had held out from me out of his hands. I was about to walk to the table before he jerked me back to him with more force than he really needed.

I looked at him with fear in my eyes and this devil smiled and kissed me on the lips, then let me go. I didn't know what kind of game he was playing, but it wasn't fun for me.

I hated living in fear every day of my life. That was one of the reasons I turned to Christian. I could tell that he could protect me if need be. He had this aura about him when I met him, one that said fuck with me if you want to. That was why I went so hard to get his attention.

I needed a man that would take me away from this hell and protect me when the psycho came for me because I knew that he would. If only I had a man like Christian. I told him that I was okay with our arrangement because I had a lot to lose too, but that was a lie. I just needed him to fall for me and take me away from all of this.

"How was your day?" he asked while taking a sip of champagne.

"It was okay, how was yours?"

"It was going good until I went by your job to surprise you and they said that you had left for the day." He looked me in the eyes like he was waiting on me to lie.

I had to think quick because there was no way that I could tell him that I was cheating on him; I would surely die tonight. "Then I came home and you weren't there either. Where were you?"

I had to make sure that I choose my words wisely because if I said the wrong thing, he was gonna go upside my head. I could play the 'I don't know what happened to us, we used to be so happy' role, but the last time I did that, I got slapped across the couch. Maybe this time would be different.

"I just needed to clear my mind, so I went to the park and watched the kids play and thought about things."

I threw the kids in there because I wanted kids and he didn't, at least right now.

"Things like what?" He put his glass down, took a step towards me and I jumped. "I'm not going to hit you, chill out. Plus, we have an event coming up and I need you fresh and beautiful."

Did he really just say that? He was not going to beat me

today because he needed me for an event. I should show my ass so that he can whoop my ass and not have to go the fucking event.

"Just us," I dropped my head and turned on the theatrics. "We used to be so happy, you and I. Now it's like all we do is fight."

I sniffled and he grunted, but he hadn't hit me yet so I guess that was a good thing.

"I just want to be like we were."

"What, broke and living paycheck to paycheck?" he huffed.

"At least we were happy and you weren't beating my ass every other day."

He rushed me and grabbed my throat. I closed my eyes to prepare me for the beating that was sure to come.

I felt his breath on my ear and he whispered, "Let's eat."

He walked to his side of the table and sat down then looked up at me. He looked down at the chair, signaling for me to sit down.

I sat down and looked at him. I said a quick prayer to God that he wasn't trying to poison me.

"Nothing is wrong with the food. If I wanted you dead, you would be dead already."

I just looked at him and said another quick prayer that I made it through this night. I needed to get away from him, and quick. I didn't know how much longer I would be able to do this.

Chapter Four

MESSIAH

I didn't know what the fuck Christian was fucking doing, but I wanted to fuck him up for it. He called me whining and shit, talking about how he fucked up and shit. I told him to meet me at the ring. I worked out at this gym that had a boxing ring in it, and I was going to show his ass a little something for being so fucking dumb.

Ivy and Reign were the best things to ever happen to us. I swear they were. Before they came along, we were out here doing reckless shit, not giving a damn about nothing. Fucking random bitches and just not giving a fuck. Since they stepped in to the picture, they have given our lives some meaning. We were just drug dealers out here trying to make a sale. We were about to be businessmen with wives and kids.

I knew my man was still caught up on that abortion shit, but he had to get over that. She made a mistake and now she was about to have his junior. Why in the hell he wanted to stress her out was beyond me. But if he didn't get his shit together soon, I was going to fuck him up.

His shit had even boiled over into my house. He had Reign questioning me because Ivy was questioning her, and I hated that shit. I prided myself on being a loyal person and when someone questioned that, it pissed me off. I had to remind myself of what was going on daily so I didn't snap on Reign for the bullshit she was pulling, like calling my phone a thousand times while I was out working, or asking me who I was with when I was not with her. Our relationship was built on trust and just because they were keeping secrets from each other didn't mean shit with us. Hopefully after this go round in the ring, Christian would get his fucking sense back.

"Aight babe, I'll be back," I yelled to Reign.

"Where are you going?"

Here she goes with this shit.

"To the gym with the guys and you know that shit already, so why are you asking me things you already know, Reign?"

"Damn, I just asked a question Messiah!"

"No, you're trying to see if I'm gon' lie."

"Anyway, we need to talk."

"About?"

"This strip club that you don't think I know about."

She put her hands on her hips and looked at me like she dared me to lie.

Fuck, how in the hell did she know about that?

"I wasn't hiding it from you; I just didn't tell you because I didn't know if it was going to go through."

"That's bullshit, Messiah, and you know."

"Look, we will talk about this later."

"No, we won't. We will talk about this before you leave this house or we gon' have problems you ain't ready for."

I was getting irritated. I didn't want to talk about this right now because I knew for a fact this was going to be an argument. But what Reign wanted Reign got, so I was going to tell her what she wanted to hear.

"Aight, look. I was approached by this lawyer that I work with." She understood what I meant when I said 'worked with'. "He said that opening a club would be a great way to clean up some of the money that we make. Because outside of you, Ivy's business, and Shamaad's car washes, that's all we got to clean up this money. With a club, it will be easy."

"Why not open a restaurant or a sports bar; why does it have to be a strip club, damn?"

"Strip clubs make the most money, and they make quick money."

"I don't want to hear that shit. I'll tell you what, you want more kids, kill that strip club idea. I'll be damned if I'm home with a thousand kids while you're at the club wilding out of control."

"Don't start that dumb shit, Reign."

"As far as I'm concerned, the conversation is over."

She strutted her hostile ass up the stairs like she ran something. I had half the mind to run up those stairs and give her little ass some act right, but instead, I was going to take all of my anger out on Christian in the ring.

"We will talk about this when I get back!" I yelled up the stairs after her, just to let her know that I ran shit.

The conversation wasn't over until I said so. All I heard was the door slam.

I just shook my head and headed out the door to the gym.

The gym was unusually empty today. Normally you would have to fight for machines and put in reservations for the rings. Not today, though. I was happy about that because we could all talk freely about life.

One by one, the guys started straggling in. I swear they were worse than the females when it came to being on time. Shamaad and the twins were the first ones to get there.

"Yo, I need to get in the ring with Christian's ass," Shamaad said, jumping around, shadow boxing with his damn self. "I'm tired of arguing over his lying ass."

"What the fuck are you talking about, Shamaad?" Raheem asked.

"Ivy's ass keeps calling Jess about the shit they going through, and that shit starting to piss me off. I pulled my gun on her ass before I left."

"Why in the fuck are you pulling guns on your ol' lady, fool?" Shaheed asked.

"Because I told her if she questions me one more time I was gon' pull it out on her. After I told her where I was going, her phone rang and it was Ivy. They talked for a little bit, and when they got off the phone, Jess asked who was going with us. I told her ass."

"Yo, yo, yo, what's up fellas?" Christian waltzed in like he didn't have a care in the world. Every last one of us wanted to fuck him up and it showed. "What the fuck wrong with y'all?"

"You, nigga," was all I said. "Just suit up; we're going first."

I needed to take all of my frustrations out on this nigga and I planned to do just that. We both got our shit on and got in the ring. The dude that usually trained me in the ring was the acting referee. He told us the rules, which I paid no attention to.

We touched gloves and I went to work. I hit Christian with a two piece that left his ass dazed, but I knew that he wasn't going to take this shit lying down. He came back with a powerful jab to the jaw. I figured now was a good time to tell him why I was about to whoop his ass.

"Do you know how much shit you have caused, nigga?"

Christian swung, I ducked and came up with an upper cut.

"Everybody is arguing with their ladies and shit because of your fuck ups."

"Y'all shit ain't got nothing to do with me."

"See partner, that's where you're wrong."

I started beasting on him. Blow after blow and I wasn't stopping either. He was keeping up at first, but after a while, his ass got tired and just went to the ropes and covered himself. I was taking everything that I was feeling out on him. I needed him to understand that his actions affected other people, especially when we were all as close as we were.

Dude finally came and pushed me back. Christian stood up, rushed me and I hit him with a hard-right hook. He landed on his ass. He jumped up and started taking off his gloves, so I followed suit.

"Nah, y'all stop that shit." Shaheed jumped up and jumped in the ring with us. "We ain't having none of that shit."

"That's right. We're brothers, nigga."

Raheem looked back and forth between us.

Christian was standing there like a raging bull.

I just looked at that nigga because I was feeling just how he was looking.

"Fuck this, I'm gone."

Christian jumped out of the ring and grabbed his shit, but Shamaad jumped in front of him.

"Nah bruh, we gon' talk about this shit."

Shamaad was trying not to laugh because his ass thought everything was funny.

Shamaad pushed Christian back because he was still trying to leave. Christian bucked at Shamaad and he jumped into a karate stance.

"I will karate chop yo' dick off, nigga. Come on."

Christian was trying so hard not to laugh, but it didn't make it any better when we all laughed. Shamaad's ass was a fucking clown, but we could always count on him to make shit better though.

"Look, y'all don't know how that shit felt when the woman that you thought was your everything, the one you loved and trusted with your all, jumps and kills yo' seed. That shit ain't happened to none of y'all, so you don't know what the fuck was going through my head."

He was right. I never experienced that shit, and I don't know what the fuck I would have done had Reign done some shit like that, but that still don't give him the right to go out and fuck some random and make shit worse.

"Nigga, you forgave her!" I yelled at him and his body language went into defense mode. "Do you plan on leaving her? Do you plan on living your life without her? Huh, nigga?"

"Fuck you, Messiah."

"You been doing enough of that shit for all of us."

Christian tried to rush me and I was ready for him. It looks like that little beating his ass got wasn't enough.

All the guys jumped in front of us and were trying their best to keep us apart.

"You're supposed to be my brother man, and you're sitting here sounding like a bitch."

"No, you sound like a bitch! Y'all don't know what I been through, she hurt me," I mocked him. "You know that girl didn't do that shit on purpose. If you gon' be with her, then do that, and stop this dumb shit. 'Cause while yo' ass out here doing what the fuck you want, we're all here taking the heat for yo' dumb ass. Got us fighting with our women like we the ones out here fucking. Get yo' shit together, bruh. You're making shit hard for all of us."

Christian jerked away from Shamaad again and Shamaad pushed him. He dropped his bag and then sat down on the bench and put his head in his hands. Christian knew he was wrong. It was just hard for him to admit it, because his pride was all in the way.

"Y'all, I fucked up."

"Nahhhhhh nigga, you think?" Raheem and Shaheed said at the same time.

"No, for real. I told her that I wanted to be single, but I don't mean that shit. I was just so tired of her questioning me and shit."

"Nigga, yo' ass cheating, the fuck," Shamaad's ass said.

"That's not the point. She wouldn't shut up, kept talking about how I was out here doing single shit, then she was about to let me be single or some shit. I told her that maybe that's what I wanted." He shook his head and I wanted to hit his ass again. "I didn't mean that shit. Ivy is my world; I could never see my life without her."

"Then you better fix this shit and now, 'cause I'm tired of arguing with Reign because she thinks I'm covering for you."

"Me too, nigga," Shamaad let him know.

"Aight y'all, I get it, damn!"

We all talked for a little bit more and hugged it out. This was the normal for us. We would fight like hell and make up in the same sentence. I just needed to get him to understand that his actions affected all of us just like if were out there in the streets and he made a bad decision, we would all pay for it. Everybody had left except for me and Christian. We had walked to the car and we were just standing there.

"You need to tell her."

"I don't know how to tell her man; I can't lose her."

"If you don't tell her, and she finds out from someone else, its gon' be even worse."

He already knew that. That was why he just stood there staring off in to space.

"Christian, TELL HER!"

"Aight, aight, I'ma tell her." He finally looked at me. "I'm sorry, bruh, I didn't know that shit was that bad."

"You good, just fix that shit! But check it. I got something that I want to show you, follow me."

Chapter Five

CHRISTIAN

I followed Messiah to wherever the hell he was taking me. As mad as I wanted to be about their little intervention they tried to have with me today, I knew they were only looking out for me that. They probably weren't getting any pussy behind this shit I had caused. I really needed to get my head together before I fucked around and lost Ivy's ass for good.

The look in her eyes the other night killed me. How could I be so stupid as to tell her some shit like that knowing good and damn well I didn't want to be single. I wanted a life with her and I was going to do everything in my power to do so.

We pulled up next to a construction site that was in the middle of downtown Charlotte on one of the busiest streets in the city and got out. I looked up at the partially finished building, and the sign across the top read Club Dynasty. It hit me that we were standing in front of the strip club that Messiah was about to open.

"Damn, this shit is going to be nice." I couldn't take my eyes off the massive size of the building. "You're about to do the damn thing with this shit."

"We," he said and I looked at him like he was crazy.

We had just talked about the shit that Eileen and I were going through. He knew good and damn well that I was not going to be able to go in with him on no damn strip club.

"I changed the concept of the club. I'm not gon' do no strip club, we just gon' make it one hell of a night spot. I'm talking three levels and a balcony, and each level plays different kinds of music. The top level is VIP only and they gotta pay to be up there. We'll have some cage dancers in there and everything. It's gon' be big and I want you in there with me."

I thought about what he was saying for a minute and I was getting excited at just the thought of owning a club. Fuck, I was in. Hopefully, this would score some kind of brownie points with Ivy.

"Fuck it, you don't have to convince me. I'm in."

We dapped up and hugged it out.

I was starting to feel good about life for a second until I heard my name being called. Great, that was the last thing I needed was for her to show up here and someone else see her out here.

"What the fuck are you doing here, Keri?"

"You won't return my calls and I just needed to talk to you," she said, looking between me and Messiah like she didn't want him standing there. "Can we talk in private?"

"Fuck no, what the fuck do you want?"

"I mean you just pretty much dropped me like I wasn't shit. How we go from seeing each other damn near every day for two whole weeks to you not answering the phone."

Was she serious right now?

I looked over at Messiah, who was shaking his head and looking down at his watch, telling me to hurry this shit up.

I didn't understand her thought process because she knew I had a girl just like I knew she had a husband, so I just didn't know what the problem was. The last time I saw her, I thought we had an understanding.

"I thought you understood shit from the beginning. You told me that you were cool with this just being a short-term thing. You already knew about Ivy and you know I ain't about to leave her for nobody, especially not you."

"What is that supposed to mean?"

She looked offended, but at this point I didn't care because she was pissing me the fuck off. "So you mean to tell me that you didn't feel anything the whole time we were together?"

"You mean besides the back of your throat? Hell naw."

That made Messiah laugh and Keri pissed.

"We fucked around for two weeks, two fucking weeks!

There is no way in God's green earth you could have fallen head over hills for me that quick. I know I can slang the hell out of some pipe, but that shit shouldn't have you acting like this."

"That's fucked up," was all she said before she walked away in the opposite direction.

"What the fuck was I thinking?" I asked no one in particular.

"I been asking myself the same got damn question since you told me the shit."

"Let me get out of here. I'm about to go buy Ivy some shit and take it home to apologize. That shit right there just reminded me why I hated being fucking single."

Messiah started clapping his hands and shit, being smart. "You go do that. I'm going home to put a baby in Reign just to piss her off."

"Aight, bruh." We dapped up and headed to our cars. Right before we got to our respective vehicles, I turned to Messiah, "Thanks for today, I needed that."

"Clearly!" he laughed and we both got in the car.

I ran by the jewelry store and then to the florist. I wanted to make sure that Ivy knew just how sorry I was. I planned on telling her what the fuck I did and then beg for her forgiveness. I prayed on everything that she didn't leave me.

I got home and noticed that her car was there and I was grateful. I walked in the house and didn't see her downstairs, so I headed upstairs to see if I could find her.

As soon as I hit the top of the stairs, I heard the shower running. My dick immediately got hard. All I wanted to do was play inside her but I know that I shouldn't, not before I told her what happened.

I walked into the spare bedroom, where she had been staying since our little fight. I sat on the bed and laid out everything that I had bought for her on the bed. I wanted her to see it when she walked out of the bathroom.

I had to get myself together before she came out because my body was reacting to her scent even more than it had when I walked up here. I took a few deep breaths and looked around the room. She had really moved into this room. Her lotions that usually lined the dresser in the room were now in here, and her favorite blanket that she used to nap with was in here. I had to fix this because this shit wasn't life.

"Ahhhhh!" she screamed when she walked out of the bathroom naked as the day she was born. "What the hell, Christian?"

"I wanted to talk to you about some shit," I said as I turned to grab the stuff that I bought for her.

I handed it to her and she just looked at it.

"You think this is going to make the way you have been acting just go away?"

"No, I'm not trying to make it just go away. I just want you to know how sorry I am and that I will never say no shit like that again."

I had so much more to say, but my words got caught in my

throat. Ivy hadn't bothered covering up. Instead, she stood in front of me with her leg hiked up on the chair, her belly protruding, and I could see her freshly shaven pussy. "I'm sorry, but I can't help it."

"Christian, what—" was all that she was able to get out before I was on my knees in front of her with my lips latched around her clit. "Ummmm, stop, I'm mad at you."

"Well, let me help you get un-mad."

I threw her leg over my shoulder and ran my tongue the length of her pussy until I felt her sweet nectar coat my tongue. That gave me the go ahead that I needed. I stood up and directed her to the bed. I laid her down gently, spread her legs as far as they could go, and just nibbled on her clit for a minute.

"Ooooooo, oooooo shit, Chris," she moaned out.

"You like that, baby?" I teased.

She didn't say anything. She just threw her head back and started throwing her pussy in my face just like I liked it. I made circles, causing her to do the same thing with her hips, then I focused in on her clit. I did that a few times until I felt her about to cum. Then, I covered her clit with my mouth and sucked it as if my life depended on it.

"Ohhhh, sssssss, yessssssss, I'm about to cum, ooohhhhh shitttttttt."

I continued to suck her dry until she started fighting me to let her up. I always thought that was funny. When she couldn't take anymore, she would scratch at my hands and swing at the back of my head until I stopped. That only made me go harder. I got back right into my groove. I needed her to cum at least three more times so that I could get her ready for what I was about to tell her. I know that shit wasn't right, but I had to do what I had to do.

"Ummmm, stop Christian, I gotta pee," she said and my head shot straight up.

I wanted to see if she was for real. I wasn't sure and I damn sure was not about to chance that shit. So I jumped up and let her go and she ran to the bathroom.

"You can leave now, Christian, and take that shit with you. I cannot be bought. When you learn how to be the man that I fell in love with again, then we can talk, but I don't know who you are right now."

I had to stand there for a minute because there was no way that she was about to leave me sitting her with blue balls and nut on my face. I really needed to talk to her.

"Ivy, we need to talk. That was foul as hell what you just did."

"Can you leave, please? I don't want to talk right now. I'm already stressed out, just please let me rest."

She was playing the hell out of that card and I really didn't have a choice but to leave her alone. She needed to rest and I didn't want anything to happen to my baby, so I let her go.

I walked to my bathroom and cleaned my face off, washed my hands and brushed my teeth. I needed to get out of the house before I went in that room and raped my pregnant girlfriend.

I walked by the room and I could hear her on the phone. I

stopped to listen and overheard her making reservations at a hotel with her sneaky ass. I let her go ahead and make reservations and I would find out exactly which hotel. As soon as she got checked in, I was going and dragging her ass right back home.

I couldn't believe I had let him touch me. I had been doing so good, and then I just had to let him touch me. With the way I was feeling, I needed to get out of the house at least for tonight, because he had my hormones raging and I knew Christian all too well. If he smelled my pussy getting wet, he would be right there in my damn face like he just was. I should have never been fucking with him like that. I should have gone and put on some damn clothes, but no, I just had to parade around naked and shit.

I called the Ritz-Carlton on East Trade to get me a room for the night. I didn't care what he said, I was getting out of there tonight. I couldn't be around him right now. I would leave a note and let Reign, who I'm sure would tell Messiah, know exactly where I was going to be.

I laid back on the bed and just thought about my life.

How the fuck did I get to this point? I thought that Christian and I would be like Reign and Messiah, somewhere happily married. I guess that wasn't in the cards for me right now.

I sat around and waited until I heard the door shut. After I was sure that he was gone, I started packing my bags and left the house.

I drove to the hotel in silence. I had so much on mind that I couldn't grasp it all. I felt like my life was falling apart. Here I was nine months pregnant, and running from my baby's father. I just wanted to be happy, but I was so scared that that was not going to happen with Christian.

I pulled up to the valet. They helped me out of the car and grabbed my bags. I went to check in and get comfortable.

The Ritz was such a nice hotel. The room that I was in was decorated in burgundy and gold. The bed was a king-sized sleep number bed that I turned mid-way, so it wouldn't be too soft and not too firm, but just right.

I could feel myself dozing off and then my phone had to ring.

"Hello?"

"You can kill the attitude, I just wanted to warn you that yo' crazy ass baby daddy is on his way to the Ritz to drag yo' ass home."

"What?!" I jumped up out of the bed. "I left him a note saying that I needed to get away for one damn night. Damn, I just need to clear my mind for one fucking night."

Knock! Knock! Knock!

Fuck! I already knew who it was, so I went and opened the door and walked away.

I hopped back on the bed and talked to Reign as if he wasn't even there.

"Can you pass me the remote please?"

He just looked at me like I was crazy. He picked up his phone, pushed some buttons and then put it back in his pocket. Moments later, I could hear Messiah cussing Reign out for being in our business.

"Tell Christian that was a bitch move. Be careful, boo. I gotta go before the big bad wolf blows the fucking house down."

I laughed because they were so fucking cute.

"I got your big bad wolf! Take your ass up the stairs, so I can give yo' ass something to tell," I heard Messiah.

"Bye, Ivy," Reign giggled.

"Bye, nasty asses."

I put my phone on the end of the table and Christian walked over and snatched it.

"Can I have my phone please?"

"Fuck no. Get your shit and let's go home."

The bass he had put in his voice made me so mad that I picked up the remote and hauled it at him.

"No, you go home! I told you that I needed a break for a second. I just need to clear my head for one night, and you can't even give me that, huh? Damn, I don't ask for much. Just give me that."

"Throw something else at me, Ivy."

He was huffing like he was mad, but I didn't give a fuck.

"You can clear your mind at home. Let's go."

"NO!" I yelled. "I'm not going anywhere. I'm sleeping right here on this sleep number bed."

"Well, I guess I am too."

He took his shoes off.

"Christian, look. You have been treating me like shit for the past two months, pulling disappearing acts and shit, and you just want me to be okay with it, but I'm not. I just want one night to myself without being near you."

"You can do that shit at home in the spare bedroom."

I hated his stubborn ass sometimes.

"Or, I can get this adjoining room right here and you can have your time and I will be right next door. I won't bother you, but I will know that you are safe. You are too far along to be trying to pull that 'I wanna be by myself' shit, Ivy."

I had never even thought about the fact that I was pregnant and I could go into labor any day now. I guess he made sense.

I took the cover that was at the bottom of the bed and threw it at him. I pointed to the living portion of the suit I was in. It had a pull-out sofa that he could sleep on.

"The couch though?"

"YEP!" With that, I retrieved the remote and started flipping channels while waiting on the room service that I ordered.

I was determined to get some peace, even if I had to pretend he wasn't here.

Chapter Seven

TY

I sat and watched as Ivy got out of her car and walked over to the entrance of her office. Even pregnant, she was beautiful. I hated the day she found out about my wife. I wish that I could spend my life with her. I just needed a little more time and I would have found a way to break it off with Tyesha.

Me and my wife hadn't been happy in years, which was why I started bringing women in the bedroom with us. She loved that; it was like it woke something up inside of her. We used to do all kinds of things, and for a while I loved it, but after a while, I felt like I needed more and she wasn't ready to stop. It had gotten to the point that she would go and bring the women home herself.

After I met Ivy, I had no interest in anything else. Eventually, I stopped participating and that was what caused the problems in our situation.

When I met Ivy, she was different. I didn't want to share her with anyone. I wanted her to be all mine, which was why I went through the lengths I did to try and carry on a full-fledged relationship with her.

The day that Ivy found out about my wife and kids was one of the worst days of my life. I swear when I saw her in the mall my stomach dropped to my feet, and my life flashed before my eyes. I wished like hell I would have answered my phone the moment I saw her call. I could have dodged her or something so that she wouldn't have seen me.

It was too late now. She was with that thug. I wanted so badly to kill him, but I had a funny feeling that if I killed him, my family nor myself would last very long on this earth. Even though I somewhat hated my wife, I loved my kids and I loved the mother that she was to them, so to keep them safe, I tucked my inner thug away.

I looked down at the envelope in my hands and I hoped like hell this would do what I needed it to do. I was hoping that she would look at these pictures of her beloved and come crawling back to me. At least that's what I was wishing.

I had been watching Mr. Christian for two full weeks. I watched him meet up with this girl in the hotel around the block from the bank. It was always the same hotel, the Marriott right by her job. There were so many times I wanted to jump out of my car and slap the shit out of him for being so stupid. I wanted to tell him that he was making the worst mistake of his life, but that was what I wanted him to do. If my plan went accordingly, Ivy would be back in my arms in no time.

I actually went into the bank and had a talk with the pretty little thing that he had been rolling around with. She was a really cool girl, and she was so open with their relationship when I told her who I was. She asked me if we could work together to break them up and I told her I didn't need any help, but she insisted. Speaking of the devil, I saw that it was her that was calling me at that very moment.

"Hey, Ty?"

"Yep! What's up?"

"Nothing, I just wanted to see when you were going to take her them pictures because I stopped in on Christian a couple weeks ago and he wouldn't even talk to me. He was all about fixing his relationship with his wife. The bitch ain't even his wife."

"Watch your fucking mouth, don't you ever call her a bitch."

I didn't know why I got so fucking mad but I had, and if she was near me, I would have slapped the shit out of her.

"What the fuck is so special about her that everyone feels like they have to protect her?"

"She's an amazing woman, and the man who gets her is one lucky son of a bitch. I hate the day I lost her, that's why I am doing all that I can to get her back."

"Yeah, yeah, whatever, just let me know if this works."

I didn't bother to answer her; she was starting to get on

my nerves. She wanted that thug so bad and I didn't know why. She was married to one of the top lawyers around, yet she wanted a dope slinging thug. That shit was beyond me. Enough about her. I was on a mission to destroy a thug.

Now, I just needed to get in the office without being seen by her pit bull, AKA Reign. If she saw me, she would surely flip the fuck out and call that thug. That would probably be the end of my life and I was trying to live long enough to get Ivy back.

Operation get my woman back had officially begun.

It had been over two weeks since the fight I had with Christian and he had pulled that little eat me out and buy me gifts routine that he thought was going to make shit right. I was still sleeping in the guest room. I wasn't saying shit to him, and I wasn't going to until he got his shit together. I can't believe he came out of his mouth and said some shit like that. If his ass wanted to be single, then I would surely allow him to be. As much as I loved him, I was not in the position to be chasing any man or trying to hold on to one that didn't want to be there. It would hurt to walk away, but it would hurt even more to stay around knowing that this was not what he wanted.

I pulled up at work and wobbled into the building and ran right into Reign. When Messiah and Dad bought the building for her home health care company and the women's center, she asked if I wanted to just move my practice on the second floor. I jumped on that immediately. I loved working with her. Both of our businesses were starting to take off. Most of my clients had moved with me, so I didn't have to worry about losing money.

"Hey, big mama," Reign joked.

"Girl, I am so ready for this boy to be out of me, I don't know what to do."

"I know what you mean. MJ couldn't get here fast enough. Now this nigga talking about more babies." We both got on the elevator. "I told him that when he shuts that strip club shit down, then I will open up shop."

"Girl, you know you're wasting your breath. You have no say so in the matter and you know it."

I don't even know why she trying to act all hard. She knew good and damn well that if Messiah wanted a baby, he would get a baby.

"Anyway, how are things with Christian?"

"I don't know."

"What do you mean you don't know, you ain't talked to the man?"

"Nope, what do I need to talk to him for? We went to the doctor the next day and I was ready before him, so I drove my own car. When he got there, he was so pissed off," I laughed.

To me the situation was funny. I didn't know why he thought shit was cool because it wasn't. "Then afterwards, he gon' try and hold a conversation with me in the parking lot. I looked at him like he was crazy, got in my car and pulled off.

He has been trying to talk to me since all of this went down and I just don't have much to say."

"What did he say when you asked him was he cheating?"

"He pretty much told me that he wanted to be single, then once he realized what he said, he tried to take that shit back and I was not having it."

"He probably said that out of anger. You know he didn't mean that."

"You didn't see his face."

I remember the look on his face when he yelled that to me; it was a look of guilt and I was sure that he was cheating, but I didn't have proof. "The nigga cheating and we will know for sure soon, because I hired Amya to bug his phone."

"Ivy, you did not do that!"

"Yes, I did! And don't you tell Messiah shit."

"This is just all too much," Reign put her hands on her hips and shook her head.

"Who you telling! I'm over this and I'm pissed that he wants to do this while I'm pregnant."

The abortion was a bit much, and like I had said before, I would take full responsibility for that. When we talked about it, he should have told me that he would not be able to get over it; we could have gone about things differently. We could have set it up so that we could co-parent and everything else be done with.

"Look, just stop stressing and take care of my nephew, everything else will fall into place."

I got up, hugged her and watched as she strutted out of

my office like she was walking in a runway show. My sister was a baddie and she knew it.

I got all of my things ready for my day. I talked to my receptionist to see what the rest of my week looked like because this was my last week before I went on maternity leave. I had a colleague that was going to help me out with some of my "emergency appointments." Everyone else had my number in case they needed me while I was out on leave.

My first appointment flew by like a breeze. It was a couple that had lost the spark in the relationship because the husband had cheated, and then the wife retaliated, so neither one trusted each other anymore, and their sex life was badly affected by it. They were making huge strides to get better, and I loved that they were both willing to participate to get things back right. It made me think of my situation. I wished like hell me and Christian could get it together before the baby came, but something was telling me that this mess was just the calm before the storm.

Knock! Knock! Knock!

There was a knock at the door and I told them to come in. When the person walked in, I instantly got pissed. I hadn't seen Ty in months, so I wasn't sure what his reasoning for being here was. I would admit that he looked so good in his fitted jeans and button down, but I could still see his lies behind his eyes. I couldn't believe he was standing here in my office right now like he belonged here.

"What the fuck are you doing here, Ty?" I asked through gritted teeth.

"I just wanted to see you and see how you were doing. It's been a while. I miss you."

"Nigga, go miss your wife," I raised my voice slightly, then I remembered where I was.

"We're divorced," he said and threw the divorce papers on my desk like that was going to matter. "She married another woman."

He looked at me and he kind of looked hurt.

I thought the shit was funny as fuck. That's what he gets for bringing other women into his bed, now one of them had gotten his wife.

Let me stop being petty.

"What does that have to do with me? I have moved on and it's a wrap for anything that you and I ever had. The minute you lied to me that crushed anything that we could have ever been."

"But your baby daddy making hotel runs with some chick from the bank, and you're okay with that? What the fuck is the difference, Ivy?"

Aggravation was evident in his voice, but I didn't give a fuck. I was still on the part where he said that Christian was fucking bitches from the bank.

"What the fuck did you just say?"

I cocked my head to the side because I was two seconds from reaching my hand in my desk drawer and giving him something he'd been missing—a bullet to the fucking forehead. "How do you know what the fuck Christian has been doing?"

"Calm down, Ivy."

He looked worried, as he should be.

"DON'T TELL ME TO CALM DOWN," I yelled. "WHAT THE FUCK ARE YOU TALKING ABOUT?"

I grabbed my stomach because I felt like I was having Braxton Hick contractions again. I knew all of this stress wasn't good for my baby, and if anything happened to my baby, Christian was gonna take his last breath.

"It's not what you think," he put his hands up in surrender. "I was at the credit union depositing money and I saw him outside of the bank. Right as I was about to turn around and get back in my car because I didn't want any issues with him, I saw a beautiful woman come out and get into the car with him."

"Okay, that could have been anybody, or business for that matter," I said, trying to defend him, even though something in my gut was telling me what he was saying was true.

"I followed them to the Marriot. They were in there about three hours, and then they came out and he dropped her back off at the bank."

He dropped his head and then looked up at me again. "I went to the bank the next day to deposit the money I never got to deposit, and it was around the same time because I was just getting off work, and he was there again. This time, she got in her car and followed him to the same hotel."

I wanted to break down, but I couldn't do that in front of Ty. I just looked at him with the evilest look.

He reached in his back pocket, pulled out a folder and

handed it to me. It was pictures that he had taken from the different days that he saw them together. I had to give it to Christian, the girl was cute, but she wouldn't be for long.

"This is proof for the last couple of weeks. I don't know how long it's been going on, but this is what I have seen."

"So what do you plan on getting out of this?" I wanted to know his motive. "Because even if I leave Christian today, I will still never be with you."

He looked defeated; all that work for nothing. People kill me, can't wait to bring someone down so they can take their spot. But there was no spot to take; I was done with all men at this point.

"Thank you for everything. If you would please let yourself out, I would greatly appreciate it."

"Ivy, all I want is a conversation to explain myself. I'm not asking for a commitment. I just want a chance to get things back on track with you, even if it's just being your friend for right now."

"I need time to think, Ty," I shook my head. "I need you to leave."

"Okay, but I hope to hear from you." He laid a card on my desk. I didn't even pay it any attention, I just laid my head down on the desk. "I still love you, Ivy."

I did not lift my head from the desk until I heard someone clear their throat.

I looked up into the most handsome face. I smoothed down my now shoulder length hair, and started to clear the things off my desk. He seemed to be enthralled with the woman in the picture.

I hurried and put them away and stood to greet him.

"I'm sorry for the mess," I reached my hand out to shake his, but he grabbed my hand and kissed it. I slowly pulled my hand back.

"I'm Dr. Ivy Richards. Will your spouse be joining us today, or will this be an appointment for just you?"

"Looks like my wife does just fine in the sex department," he said this under his breath, but I heard him.

"Excuse me?"

All of a sudden, I got an uneasy feeling.

"Oh, nothing, I do apologize. My name is Jerimiah Straggs, and it will be just me today."

I looked at him and noticed that he was looking at me in a sexual way, and I didn't like it. I think I needed to get him out of here. He was into those pictures like he knew someone on them. The line of work that Christian was in made me very aware of things like that. I needed to reschedule our meeting.

"I may need to reschedule our meeting."

"Please, no, I need your help." He looked sincere.

Maybe I was just being paranoid. I was letting the shit with Christian get in my head. I was a professional and I needed to act as such.

"I will pay extra."

"No, there is no need."

I got up and went and shut the door. I pulled out my tape

recorder to get ready for the conversation that we were about to have.

"What brings you here, Mr. Straggs?"

"Well, my wife is cheating on me and it's my fault."

My heart went out to him in that moment because I knew exactly what he was feeling. Christian was cheating on me and it was because of something that I'd done. The only difference was that I would not take responsibility for a grown ass man sticking his dick in another woman, I just couldn't do it.

"Why do you think it's your fault that your wife cheats?"

He went on to tell me how he worked all of the time and neglected her; she had talked to him about it, but he never changed anything. He said that their sex life had become nonexistent and they couldn't be in the same room with each other for more than an hour without arguing.

He wanted help getting things under control with his wife and with their sex life, so they could be happy again. I was happy to see a man who wanted to make his relationship work. Christian could damn sure take some lessons.

Chapter Nine

JERIMIAH

Just sitting here looking at Ivy's sexy self had my dick hard as a brick. Even pregnant, she was beautiful. I wondered if it would be inappropriate to ask her out. I had to laugh at myself because soon, she would be a free woman. I was here to get close to her so that I could let her know what her thug had been up to. I wondered if she knew that her man was laying up in hotel rooms with my wife.

Yeah, I knew all about her little adventures. I knew everything she did. The hotel that she went to was run by one of the many women I deal with on a regular basis. I had eyes everywhere, and Nicole was one of those women who would do everything in her power to get to the top, so the first time she saw Keri go in with Christian, I had pictures, his name, and phone number. I used that to do research, which led me here.

I was confused as to what the hell he wanted with my wife when he had this goddess right here. Maybe after I exposed them, she would run to my arms and we could run off into the sunset together. I was about to make partner at my firm and I wouldn't need to kiss up to Keri's crazy ass father anymore.

I was tired of him; just like I was tired of his hoe ass daughter. I used her to get where I was today. I will admit that when we first got together, I loved her and I wanted to build a life with her. Once I found out who her father was, I went in full force. He taught me all about the world of law, and controlling your woman. This man told me to beat his daughter to make sure that she would be submissive; he said that new aged women had that independent thing going on, and he wanted his daughter to be like his wife. At first I was like no, I can't do that, but then she started doing things he warned me about and I felt like she left me no choice. After a while, it just became a way of life. The man molded me to be a mini version of him. After he hired me straight out of law school, we were together all the time. I was the son he never had.

After they had Keri, his wife hemorrhaged and they had to do an emergency hysterectomy. She was never able to have kids again. That made Keith hate women in a way, because he never got his son to carry on his namesake. His family didn't believe in divorce, so he felt stuck and he treated his wife and daughter exactly the way he felt: stuck.

"Mr. Straggs? Did you hear what I said?"

"No, I'm sorry, beautiful. I was in my head."

"I said that we can meet again later this week, and it would be great if you brought your wife with you," she said, and I couldn't do anything but look at her beautifully sculpted lips and think about what they would look like wrapped around my dick.

"This week is not good for me, what about next week?"

"This will be my last week in the office for a month or so," she rubbed her belly and smiled. "It's time to deliver this little boy in here. But I have a colleague that will be able to help you until I am back in the office."

"No, I will just wait on you."

Fuck!

That was throwing a monkey wrench in all of my plans. I wanted to get the ball rolling now, but I guess I would have to be patient. I think I may try and get Miss, excuse me, Dr. Ivy Richards for myself.

"Okay, well here is my number if you need anything before we meet again. There will be charges for over the phone therapy as well."

"Of course."

I blew her a kiss and she gave me a look that I couldn't read. I just smiled. I turned to walk out. I opened the door and a sexy ass caramel woman walked in. It was like the sky opened and I saw heaven, and I couldn't help but stare. She was gorgeous.

"Have a good day, Mr. Straggs," Ivy said in a dismissive tone.

"You do the same, beautiful, and your beautiful friend too," I said, winking at the friend, who was now standing behind Dr. Ivy's chair.

She shook her head.

"Looks like I'm gonna have to visit more often."

"Looks like you wanna die too." I turned around and there stood two big ass niggas, and the one that was speaking had crazy ass grey eyes. He was clenching his jaw. I guess the sexy walker belonged to him.

"No disrespect. Dr. Ivy, I will be in contact."

"No the fuck you won't."

I looked back to the door where the men were standing, looking like they could kill me at any moment. The guy that had just spoken was the one I noticed from the pictures. He was the one fucking my wife. The nerve of him right now. "You got a few seconds to get out of here before you meet Louise."

"Christian!" Dr. Ivy yelled out.

"Don't Christian me. Y'all sitting up in here smiling and shit with this nigga, so it looks like to me y'all want a got damn show," Christian said.

"Yo, I ain't gon' to tell you to exit again, nigga," the crazy eyed guy walked towards me and I backed up and threw my hands up. I was clearly outnumbered.

"Reign, get yo' ass upstairs before I fuck you up."

"Messiah, you better calm the hell down. I can barely deal

with your bipolar ass, ain't nobody trying to add to that shit," the sexy walker said as she hugged Ivy and walked around the desk.

I guess I stared a second too long because the next thing I heard was a bullet being chambered.

I turned around and I could have shit myself.

"Put the guns down now, what are y'all thinking? This is my business!" Ivy was on the brink of tears. "I'm so sorry, Jerimiah."

Christian lowered his gun and looked at me, and then looked at Ivy. He shook his head and then ran his hands down his face. I guess he thought that I had told his little secret. He didn't have to worry about that, someone else had beat me to the punch, according to those pictures that she had when I got here.

"I didn't mean any disrespect; I just want to go home to my wife. I know Keri is worried sick."

I said that on purpose and it worked, because his face was now filled with guilt. My job here was done. I walked past the dude with the crazy eyes and slipped out the hallway. That was a close call.

Keri was going to pay for this shit.

Chapter Ten

CHRISTIAN

here was no way in the fucking world that that shit was a coincidence, that was Keri's husband. She had shown me pictures of the two of them before. I don't know why the fuck he was here, but if it is for what I thought it was for, I was going to kill him.

I looked over at Ivy. She stood there and shook her head. I looked over at Messiah and he was looking like he was about to kill Reign.

"BRING YO' ASS ON, REIGN."

He put some bass in his voice this time.

"Ugghhhhhhh, don't start this shit Messiah."

"Yo, if I say that shit again, I'ma cause a fucking scene."

"Girl, I love you and call me later," Reign said, looking at Ivy. "Let me go before I have to shoot his big ass."

"Keep fucking with me Reign, in here smiling in that nigga's face like yo' ass ain't married. Get yo' ass upstairs."

They left out of the office arguing; those two were made for each other. I constantly look at them and everything they've been through, and admire how they still made it. They're still happy. Why couldn't I get my shit together, because I needed that. I wanted that with Ivy.

My phone rang and I looked down at the screen. I noticed that it was Keri. I immediately declined and shut my phone off, giving Ivy my full attention right now.

Our whole reason for coming here was to invite them to the club that we had bought. I decided to go in with him when I found out he changed it from a strip club to a regular club. He wanted to surprise Reign and I wanted to talk to Ivy and spend some time with her, but the shit we walked in on may have just fucked that up.

"Christian, get out."

I looked at her like she was crazy. I knew I had said some fucked up shit, but enough was enough. We needed to go ahead and get this shit together because she would never live happy with anyone else. I would kill every man she tried to get close to, so we may as well just get it together.

"Shut that shit up. If anybody should be mad here, it's me. I walk in to surprise yo' mean ass and you in here making googly eyes with a patient. What the fuck, Ivy?"

"I ain't got to explain shit to you, Christian."

"What the fuck you mean, Ivy?" She was about to piss me

the fuck off. "Look, I said that shit because I was mad, you know I don't want to be with anybody but you."

"You sure about that?" she raised an eyebrow.

I just stood there looking at her because I didn't want to say the wrong thing. I needed to just man up and tell her what the fuck I did, but I didn't have the strength to do it.

"Ivy, stop with the trivia," I tried it that way.

"If you love someone, I mean really love them, you don't do things to purposely hurt them."

Her eyes were misty, but I knew that she would never let the tears fall. For some reason, she didn't feel safe being vulnerable around me, and I hated that. I wanted her to know that she could have the world with me. I guess I really wasn't going about it the best way, but that was what I was here for now, to make shit right.

"Look, I've done some fucked up shit, Ivy, some real fucked up shit. I hate myself for what I have put you through while you are carrying my seed. I need to whoop my own ass."

"You got that shit right because you are about to lose me."

She reached down, grabbed what looked like an envelope and slammed it on the table. "I can't believe that you would cheat on me."

She finally let go and broke all the way down.

I ran over to hold her, but she started swinging on me. She was landing hella hits, too. I finally got hold of both of her hands and bear hugged her.

"Ivy, I'm sorry," I whispered in her ear and she just cried.

I swear my heart dropped to my stomach. How could I do

this to her? I lifted her off the ground and turned her face towards me. "It will never happen again; I swear on my son's life that I will never hurt you again."

"I can—oh shit," she sniffled. I felt my feet sliding. I looked down and there was a puddle of water. "My water just broke."

"Fuck, where are the bags?"

She doubled over in pain and I grabbed her. I almost slipped in the watery shit.

"Baby, are the bags in your car?"

She nodded her head.

"Okay, I'm gonna sit you down and call Messiah and Reign."

She nodded again.

I called up to Reign's office, but there was no answer. I called three more times and nothing. I hit the intercom button and paged their ass over the intercom.

One minute later, the phone was ringing.

"Is she okay?" Reign sounded like she was panicking.

"Her water broke; we are heading out the door now," was all I said before I picked her up and carried her out the door.

When we hit the front door, Messiah and Reign were coming out of the stairway. We all rushed out, jumped in my truck and headed to the hospital. I was both excited and scared at the same time. I knew that Ivy was not going to forgive me that easily, but I had to make this right for the sake of my family.

"Push baby push!" Christian coached and I wanted to take his fucking head off.

"Shut the fuck up, you yellow bastard! This shit is all your fault!"

I was in so much pain that I didn't know what to do. It felt like someone was tearing my pussy wide open. By the time I got to the hospital, I was already eight centimeters and they said that it was too late for the epidural, so I had to handle all this shit.

"Baby, I know it hurts but—"

"You don't know shit but how to stick your dick where it doesn't belong!" I screamed, and I could've sworn I heard a nurse giggle. "What the fuck you laughing at? You fucked him too?"

"Ivy, cut that shit out! This is not the time or the place for this, let's just focus on getting my boy into this world. The other shit can wait."

"FUCK, AAHHHHHHHHHHHHHHHHHHHH!"

My ass was on fire. I swear this felt worse than death.

"One more push, Ivy, and his head will be out. You ready?"

I wanted to slap the fuck out of that doctor. Who the fuck is ever ready for this shit? "Puuuushhhhhhh!"

I pushed with everything I had, and then I heard the most angelic cry I think I ever heard.

Christian walked down and cut the cord; he was grinning like he had just won the lottery. He looked up at me after it was cut and mouthed the words, "Thank you". I wanted to hate him so much for what he had done, but in this moment, all I wanted to do was spend time with him and our son.

A few hours later, we were done with family bonding time and we were okayed to have visitors. The whole damn crew showed up. I had to say a quick prayer that we didn't get put out, especially after that show Shamaad put on when his twins were in here.

"Oh my goodness, look at him. He is so cute," Jess cooed.

"Jess, get back," Shamaad frowned up his nose. "Blowing yo' dick breath all over the baby."

We all laughed because he was truly an idiot.

"I can't stand your black ass," Jess shook her head.

"Yo' ass is getting brave, Powder," Shamaad said with a serious face.

"Who the fuck is Powder?" Christian asked with a confused face.

"You know that pasty ass nigga on that one movie."

Once I realized what the hell he was talking about, I couldn't do anything but laugh. I laughed so hard that I think I may have ripped a stitch or two. Poor Jess. I didn't know how she put up with that fool on a daily basis. I swear I would have had to shoot him and plead temporary insanity. His mouth was just too reckless.

We all joked around and hung out until the nurse came in and told everybody that visiting hours had been over for a while and that everybody needed to leave.

Christian went outside to walk everyone out. He thought he was slick. I heard his phone going off the entire time that he was here.

If someone would have told me that day in the parking lot of Concord Mills Mall that we would be here right now, I would have told them that they were crazy. With everything that Ty had put me through, I was determined to focus on me and not another man. But here he came, Mr. Future, changing the entire game. I just wished that he would have held up his end of the bargain. Now, I was left here to decide if I could forgive him for fucking around, or whether I should do what my first mind said and leave him. The only thing about leaving him was CJ. I knew I talked all that shit about not being with him because of the baby, but now that he was here, I understood why women fought so hard for their families.

"Shamaad's ass is a fool," Christian said walking into the room and picking Christian Jr. up out of the bassinet.

"Shamaad is crazy. I feel so sorry for my girl."

"Shittin' me, Jess is just as crazy."

"Y'all make us crazy."

That comment silenced him for a second; he didn't know how to come back from that. I just wanted to hear him say that he fucked up and he would never do it again. What I wouldn't take was if he started to come out of his mouth with excuses. The only way that I would consider working on us was if he admitted that he was wrong. I couldn't even believe that the thought of staying with him was even crossing my mind after what he did, but CJ changed things. I wanted my family for him. Now, don't get shit twisted; I would not stand around while he continued to do it. The shit would end today or I would walk.

"Ivy," he started, but you could tell that he was nervous. "I'm sorry, baby. I don't know what the fuck I was thinking. You are my everything and I don't see a life without you. Please don't leave me. I will do whatever it takes to make this shit right. Only thing that matters to me in this world is you and my son. Just tell me what to do and I will do it."

"Cut all ties with that bitch. I know she works at the bank that you use. You need to go in there and withdraw everything and move banks. That's number one," I said with finality. "I just wanna know why, Christian. I love you with everything in me, how could you do this to us? You know how big I am on trust, and you go and do this?"

"I know, baby, and I'm sorry. I was just in my head about that abortion shit. I can't believe I let my got damn ego come in between me and you."

"Please stop using that as an excuse."

His face turned cold and the sentimental look in his eyes was now gone. His demeanor turned defensive.

"I'm not using shit as an excuse. That shit really hurt me. No, it didn't make me go fuck somebody else, but at the time, I just needed a release, so that's what I did. Am I proud of that shit? Hell no. If I could take that shit back I would have never done no shit like that. But I was hurt, Ivy, and hurt people hurt."

"Hurt people hurt, huh? I guess I can go out and hurt you now that you hurt me then."

"Ivy, you hurt me more than you will ever know when you killed my seed. I don't think there is anything else that you can do to me," he said solemnly, and that made me feel like shit.

I was not about to let him turn this shit around on me though. I wasn't the one that betrayed the trust in our relationship.

"But you can try that shit if you want to, I will kill every man that you attempt to date and send you their heads in a box. Now try me."

That was the last thing that he said before he walked over to the sofa that was in the room and laid down with CJ on his chest. *Crazy bastard.*

He was the one that had cheated but he was sitting here

threatening me. I still had a lot of thinking to do. I wanted to have my family, but not if he was still holding on to the fact that I had an abortion. If he was still playing on that, then we would never be right. We needed to have a serious conversation about us.

It was the night of the event and Jerimiah had been super nice to me today. I didn't know what the fuck he was up to, but I was not about to be part of it. I had been calling Christian all day, in hopes that he would pick up so that I could possibly get his help to escape this madness, but he never answered. I guess he was done fucking with me. I didn't know that I would be able to let go that easy. I knew that it had only been a couple of weeks, but I felt a connection to him and he felt one to me, whether he wanted to admit or not.

"Remember, just smile and be pretty, don't do a lot of talking. That's not what you are there for. There will be a lot of important people there tonight, and I don't need you saying something stupid."

God, I hated this man. I prayed daily that I would find

someone that would just take me away from all of this. I would make someone a good wife. Maybe if I could get Christian to see that this was where he wanted to be, he would leave Ivy and be with me.

"Did you hear what I said, Mrs. Straggs?"

The way he called me that sent chills down my spine.

"Yes, Jerimiah," was all I said, and I guess that wasn't enough because he ran up behind me and pushed me up against the wall. I just knew that he was about to beat my ass, but instead, he snatched my thong off and spread my legs. I could hear him fumbling with his belt and I wanted to question him, but I knew better. I wasn't in the mood for his few pumps and a wet ass today. I was in my feelings that I hadn't talked to Christian.

"Bend over." I did as I was told while he jammed his fingers into my still dry vagina. "Oh, you can't get wet for me anymore?" His voice was harsh and cold. "I don't do it for you anymore, Keri?"

If I didn't know any better, I would have thought that his ass was slightly offended. We barely had sex, and when we did, it was always over before we started.

I didn't say anything though, I just closed my eyes and imagine that it was Christian's hands playing in my honey pot. Once I completely forgot about my husband and focused all thoughts on Christian, the gates opened up and I was immediately coating his fingers.

"Ummmmm, baby, please give it to me," I moaned out in ecstasy from the finger action I was getting. "I need you."

I felt his head at my opening and I threw my head back as he entered me nice and slow. He grabbed a fist full of my hair and gave me nice and slow strokes, causing me to gasp every time he went in. I swear I felt every inch of him. I couldn't help but to throw my ass back so that I could catch everything he was throwing my way.

"Sssssssss, just like that." I was in a world of my own and I didn't want to leave. "Nobody handles my body like you."

He sped up his motions, and all you could hear through the entire room was my moans and our skin slapping.

"Tell me how you like it," Jerimiah moaned in my ear.

My eyes popped opened and I was forced back into reality. My love box dried up almost instantly but that didn't stop him. He pounded in and out of me like I was a hooker off the street. "Fuck, I'm about to nut."

Thank you!

I was ready for him to get his and get away from me. He just had to open his mouth and take me away from my fantasy with Christian. I was starting to be obsessed with a man that belonged to another woman. I didn't know what my problem was, but I was starting to believe that I deserved better than the verbal and physical abuse that had been my life for over a decade now.

"Go shower so that we can get ready to go," Jerimiah demanded.

I was dreading going to this event because he always found a way to blame me for anything that went wrong at these things. I just wanted to stay home and chill and think about the way Christian made me cum. I wondered if I were to fake sick would he would let me stay home.

"Don't even think about backing out of this, you are going. I am not about to spend all night explaining to people why you are not there."

Fuck, I hated when he did that. It was like he always knew what I was thinking.

"No, you wore me out, that's all," I lied.

"Well, if you're a good girl, I will give you more when we get home."

He had the nerve to wink at me. Great! I done pumped his head up, and now I have to have sex with him again. That's what the hell I get for lying.

We were dressed and ready to go within the hour. We walked out of the house hand in hand like we were the couple of the year. On the outside, you would think that I was the perfect wife and him the perfect husband, but that was far from the truth.

When we arrived at the event, I could have sworn that I saw Christian's car, but I guess my mind was just playing tricks on me. We walked in like we were about to grace the pages of a magazine. Everyone stopped to speak to Jerimiah as if he was some big celebrity. He was great in his field, I would give him that, but that's where his greatness stopped.

"Well, well, well, look what we have here," my dad said as he walked over to where we were standing. "Look at my beautiful daughter."

"Hi, Dad." It came across like I was actually glad to see

him, but I was sure the look on my face said otherwise. "Where's Mom?"

"She is over there talking to the other wives," he said with a sour tone.

"Well I'm going to go join her." I started to walk in the direction that my mother was in.

"I want you to meet someone first."

My dad turned around and got the attention of the two men that were standing behind us with their backs to us. When they turned around, I had to stop the smile that was starting to spread across my face.

"This is Christian Hope and Messiah King; they are opening up one of the biggest clubs that Charlotte has ever seen. They are the people to know if you want to be successful around here. Christian and Messiah, this is my daughter Keri and her husband, and soon to be partner of the firm, Jerimiah."

Christian and the Messiah guy just sat there and stared at Jerimiah as if they wanted to kill him. I would not protest at all; they would be doing me a favor if they just did away with him. Jerimiah reached out his hand. They both looked down at his hand and then turned to walk away. Christian never even looked my way, but I guess he just didn't want to give us away.

"Christian, is there a problem?" my dad asked.

"Just keep that bitch ass nigga away from my wife," was all that Christian said before he walked off.

He was pissing me off with this wife stuff. I didn't know

why he kept referring to her as his wife. He told me himself that he didn't know if he would marry her because of what she did.

"What is he talking about, son?" My dad had a questioning look on his face.

"Nothing. His wife is a sex therapist and I went to talk to her about my marriage, and when my appointment was over, he showed up waving guns in the air and stuff. I never said two words to him," Jerimiah said.

"Well, you need to fix that shit! I'm trying to get them to put the firm on retainer." My father rubbed his hands together. "Do you know what that would mean for the firm if he puts his whole team on?"

I looked in the direction that Christian had walked, and then back at my father. I didn't know what the hell he was talking about. What the hell did he do for a living that would cause him to have to have a team of lawyers at his disposal?

"I take it y'all don't know shit about them." My dad shook his head. "They are the biggest drug dealers North Carolina has ever seen. Their legacy will be talked about for years to come."

"They are criminals," Jerimiah said with his nose turned up.

"For you to be so smart, your ass sure is dumb. What the fuck do you think you do for a living? What in the entire hell do you think pays your bills and affords you to live the life that you are living right now?" My father waited for an answer, but all he got was silence. "I'll answer it for you, by defending criminals."

My father walked off in the direction that Christian and Messiah had gone. He shook their hands and the Messiah guy looked over to where we were standing. He looked directly at me. His stare was so cold that it caused me to get a cold chill. I had to look away. He was starting to scare me.

"Do you see what you've done?" I just looked at him and wondered what story he was about to come up with that would make this my fault. "We will talk about this when we get home."

He walked off to go mingle with the other patrons and I walked over to the women, making sure that I had a clear sight of Christian. I watched as a few women walked over to where him and Messiah were standing. They smiled and talked for a few but from a distance. Messiah made sure that every woman that walked in his sight could see that shiny ass wedding band. You could tell that he loved and respected his wife. That's what I wanted. Now only if I could get Christian to see that I could be that.

Christian took off to the bathrooms and I followed, making sure that Jerimiah didn't see me following him. He was over on the other side of the room, cheesing all in some other woman's face. That was nothing out of the norm with him. He thought that I didn't know about the many women, but I did. I knew about all of them because they never failed to let me know how often they fucked my husband. From the sounds of what they said, they are damn sure getting way more than what I was getting, which was why I was following another man to the bathroom.

I posted up right outside of the men's bathroom, waiting on Christian to come out. I heard someone talking in the bathroom so I put my ear to the door. I heard him laugh.

"Awww, what are you doing to my son, Ivy?"

She must have said something funny because he laughed again. "I will be home soon, I'm about to leave now. I just gotta have the meeting with this guy and I'm done." He paused to let her speak. "I told you that I didn't want to leave y'all anyway, but you told me to come. Aight, girl, chill out with that shit. I love yo' mean ass." He started to laugh again and I swear I wanted to cry tears when he told her he loved her. "Tell Reign I ain't telling Messiah shit. Bye."

I jumped back away from the door so that he wouldn't know that I was listening. I couldn't help the defeated look that I was sure donned my face. I took a few steps back as to make it look like I was just walking up as he walked out.

When he opened the door and saw me walking his way, he dropped his head. That shit hurt more than hearing him tell his woman that he loved her.

"Well, hello Christian."

"What's up, Keri?"

"Nothing, just trying to see why I haven't heard from you," I said, trying to make it seem as though I wasn't pressed that he had been ducking me. "I've been calling and texting you like crazy."

"And you should just have recognized that you have been put on the block list."

He said that as if I wasn't shit. "What do you want? You should get back out there to your husband."

I smiled on the inside just a little bit because it sounded like he was jealous.

"Are you jealous?" I walked up on him. "I saw the way that you were looking at him. You can't stand to see him with what's yours, huh?"

This nigga had the nerve to start laughing like I was on the stage of *Def Comedy Jam* or something. I didn't see shit funny. The way he looked at Jerimiah was that of a jealous man. He could act tough all he wanted, but I knew what I saw.

"You have got to be out of your rabid ass mind to think that I would *ever* be mad at another man over you," he put much emphasis on the word, ever. "I looked at that mutha-fucka like that because his ass was in my wife's office flirting and shit like I wouldn't put a hot one in him. So, if I was jealous of anything, it was that. I don't give a fuck about you, and you should know that."

"How can you say that with everything that we shared?"

"What the fuck did we share outside of a fuck that was mediocre at best?"

"Are you serious right now?"

"As a muthafuckin heart attack."

"I thought we had something, I thought you were going to leave Ivy for me?"

"Where the fuck did you get that shit from? HUH?" he yelled and I had to jump back, remembering the last encounter we had. "I never told you that shit. You need to pull your head out of LaLa Land and get back to reality. You and I will never be anything. You were a mistake at most."

I couldn't say anything. I just stood there and listened to him tell me that I wasn't shit but a no-good fuck to him. I didn't understand why I wasn't good enough to be happy. My dad hated me; he never came out and said it, but I knew that he blamed me for not being able to have a son. My husband was a piece of shit and now this. I was done being everyone's punching bag, I was about to make somebody pay.

"Yo Christian, where you at, man? Reign starting that bull-shit and we need to have this meeting so we can go," the Messiah guy said as he rounded the corner.

He must have not seen me standing there.

"Well, I was coming until this dumb ass girl stopped me, talking all stupid and shit."

"I told you not to fuck with her! That shit is yo' fault," Messiah said, pointing at Christian. "You know how hoes are, you give 'em a taste and they go fucking crazy. I tell yo' ass if she starts some shit and it boils over into the King household, I'm fucking you up! Now, let's go!"

He gave me a disgusted look and said some shit under his breath. I was convinced that that grey eyed fool was crazy. I was going to do my best to stay the fuck away from him.

"Man look, you got your husband and I got my wife. It was

fun while it lasted, but it's done. Stay away from me and my family, you got it?"

I didn't answer, so he shook his head as if he knew something that I didn't. I was going to do everything that I could to make them all pay for the pain that they had caused me.

Chapter Thirteen

CHRISTIAN

The look Keri had in her eyes was not a good one. The first time she tried to do some dumb shit, she would be a goner. Ivy and I had talked about all of this and she agreed to forgive me on the strength that I let that abortion shit go. Feeling like I was going to lose her was the wakeup call that I needed to let that shit go. I still wasn't out of the woods yet and she let me know that the first time that she thought I was doing some shit, she was gone, and I wasn't going to have that.

"Yo, you better have all of that shit out of your system," Messiah warned. "Looks like ol' girl gon' be a damn problem, and I don't know how that is gonna work with our arrangement."

"I got this, nigga."

"You better."

Messiah's big ass always thought somebody feared him. I looked at his funny looking ass and laughed. That was my brother though, and I knew that he was just looking out for me. We needed to get this meeting over with so that I could get back to my family.

"Wait," Messiah stopped in mid stride. "Did you know that was Keith's daughter?"

"Hell no I didn't. Had I known, then I would have left her ass where she was. I should have done that in the first place."

"Got that shit right. Come on, let's go find that nigga so we can get the fuck out of here."

I looked into the crowd and noticed that he was in a heated discussion with Keri. I looked around for that bitch ass husband of hers and he was entertaining some bitch that he was clearly familiar with. For a second I felt sorry for her, that was until I looked back in the direction she was standing in and the looney bitch was staring me down. I was going to have to kill her.

Keith walked towards me, and an older version of Keri walked over to where she was standing. Keri said something to her and the older lady started to smile.

I shook my head and flipped them both off. That took the smiles right off of both of their faces and caused Messiah to laugh.

"Sorry, gentlemen. Let's step outside and talk business."

Keith led the way outside. We got outside and he took out a big cigar. He knew how impatient we were so I didn't know why he was trying to prolong this conversation. His ass begged us to increase his shipment and now his old ass couldn't handle that shit. He had Albemarle, Concord, and Salisbury on lock and he copped his shit from us. He wanted to have a meeting with us about something. I hoped he wasn't trying to reduce shit because his ass was under contract.

"You know I'm an impatient muthafucka, so it's best that you go ahead and tell me what's up before I start thinking the worst."

Messiah gave him the death stare. That muthafucka had zero tolerance for bullshit. I didn't either, but Messiah was way worse than me.

"Look gentlemen, looks like I took on more than I can chew. I need to reduce my shipment."

"Contract," was all I said.

"I know that. I was thinking if I could help you, then you could help me."

"Help us with what?" I asked him.

Messiah was silent and that only meant one thing: someone was about to get hurt.

"I've got contacts in the police and FBI. I am willing to share those with you if you just reduce my shipment back."

"We got our own contacts and I'm almost sure that they can get us more info than you ever could. So, no deal."

"What do you expect me to do? My guys can't move that shit that quick."

"Why in the fuck would you make that commitment then?" Messiah took a step towards him and I had to inter-vene because we had too many witnesses. "Check it, make sure you have my money when I get to your office on Friday, or that hoe ass daughter of yours will be picking out your suit for your final goodbyes."

Keith swallowed hard. He realized that this was not a game and he had royally fucked up.

Messiah gave him one more threatening look, then he put his hands in his pocket and walked off towards the car. I don't know why people fucked with that psycho.

"Christian, is there anything that you can do for me?"

"Once his mind is made up, that's what it is. You knew you couldn't handle that much work, so why did you ask for that shit?"

"I thought my guys could handle it, but they have been slacking off."

"Well, that's when you call in reinforcements."

"What you mean?"

This muthafucka was as dumb as they come. I didn't even know why he was trying to be in the drug game, he didn't know shit about it.

"Maybe you need to put this shit down 'cause you clearly don't know what the fuck you are doing."

The look in his eye let me know that he wanted to say something, but he knew better. We had been dealing with each other for a while. He knew who Messiah and Supreme's father was and what he was about.

I turned to walk away.

"My daughter ain't what she seems to be, she will ruin you."

"You ain't gotta tell me that shit, I already know. I'm telling you now though, if she comes for my family, you will be burying her."

"You'll be doing me a favor."

I had to tilt my head to that one. How could a man tell someone to kill their own flesh and blood? Then I thought back to my sister and hit him with a Kanye shrug.

I chucked him the deuces and headed toward the car where Messiah was waiting.

"We're gonna have to kill him and his daughter, you know that, right?" was all he asked as he cranked up the car en route to my house.

"**I** can't believe I took him back, girl."

I was still shocked that I hadn't walked away and never returned. I swear I used to talk so much shit about girls who talked all that "I wanna make it work for the kids" bullshit. Now, here I was wanting to make it work for my son.

"Girl, I was praying that your mean ass wouldn't pack yo' shit and disappear."

"I thought about it." I dropped my head because I was still thinking about it. I felt like I was giving in too easy, like he would think that shit like that was okay. "Do you think I forgave him too easy?"

"No, I don't. I think people make mistakes and Christian made a mistake. A life-threatening mistake, but a mistake nonetheless. Do I believe that he would do it again? No, I don't. He loves you, Ivy, and you know that."

"Then, why would he do that to me?"

"Because I was being an asshole and I swear on everything I love that I will never hurt you again." I didn't even hear them come into the house. I wonder how much he heard. "You ain't got shit to worry about."

I wanted to believe what he was saying, but it was hard. I knew he loved me just as much as I loved him and I wanted to make our relationship work, but he had a lot to prove to me. I would not be one to stand around while he dibbled and dabbed with other bitches, I just wasn't built like that.

"I'll tell you what, fool me once, shame on you, fool me twice, shame on me, fool me three times, I'm blowing up ya house with you in it."

Everybody just looked at me like I was crazy, but I was serious as hell. If he ever hurt me again, I was blowing his ass up and then having a funeral like I wasn't the one to take his life. I was not to be played with.

"Look, baby, I get it. No need for all of that."

He had his brows all scrunched up and shit like I was the one at fault. He clearly thought I was bullshitting.

"I won't tolerate this shit. How would you feel if I went out and fuc—" was all I got out before he was in my face, daring me to finish what I was about to say.

"Try it and I will cut the muthafucka in pieces and have them delivered to you."

"On that note, let's go, Reign," Messiah said, getting up and looking at Reign like she wasn't moving fast enough for him. She rolled her eyes and got up to get MJ ready to go. "Keep rolling them eyes and I'ma give you a reason to, Reign."

"You can try and show out if you want to, you know how quick I will close up shop. Now keep talking and talk yaself out of some pussy."

I had to giggle at that, but it was cut short because Christian gave me a look that told me to shut the hell up. I guess he was still mad at the shit I said a little while ago.

"You know what happened the last time you tried that shit," Messiah grinned, and Reign flipped him off and chuckled. "Aight y'all, we will see y'all later. Remember we got the meeting for the club in the morning, nigga, don't be late."

Reign stopped in her tracks and looked at me. She was still on the fence about them opening the strip club and this was the first time of me hearing about Christian being a part of it. He was in enough shit with me and his ass was still keeping secrets.

I pushed the hell out of him. He looked at Messiah like he had just told on him. I shook my head.

"Don't fucking do that, Ivy. that's why we came to y'all's office that day. We were going to tell y'all that Messiah changed the concept of the club and I went in with him."

"What do you mean changed the concept of the club?" Reign put her hands on her hips.

"It's not going to be a strip club. It gonna be a 'Premium Club' for the elite of Charlotte. Three levels and all of that. I was going to tell you the day you was smiling all in that nigga's face."

"Bye, y'all." Reign grabbed MJ's car seat and Messiah took it from her and pecked her on the lips.

I envied their relationship sometimes. They were crazy as hell, but the love was real. Messiah would never do anything to hurt her and she was as loyal as they came. That was what I wanted for Chris and I. I just hoped we could get back there.

"Bye, girl, and kiss my baby for me."

"Aight, boo. Want to do lunch with the babies tomorrow while the guys are meeting?"

"Sounds good, and then we can hit the mall."

"Okay, boo, and Christian?"

"What's up, sis?"

"Don't make me have to shoot yo' ass." She gave him a knowing look and he just dropped his head. "And step back, you're in her personal space."

"Bring yo' ass on, Reign. You ain't gon' do shit but take this dick."

Messiah grabbed her arm with his free arm and pulled her out of the door. The whole time she was taking two fingers and pointing at her eyes and then pointing at Christian as if to say she was watching him. We both laughed and Christian walked over to the door and shut it, right as she was yelling something.

He walked towards CJ's bassinet and he just stood there looking at him. I knew what he was feeling in that moment because I did that often. It amazed me that I took part in creating his little self.

CJ started to stir, and of course Christian bent right down and picked him up. He was going to be spoiled as hell. He never even had to cry before Christian picked him up. It's like he sat and waited for him to move so he could pick him up.

"I want this, Ivy; I want all of this. I fucked up and I admit I fucked up. I will never ever do it again. The shit wasn't even worth it; nothing is worth losing this over," he waved his hands around the room. "I was in a bad head space but I swear on everything that I love that it will never happen again. Do you believe me?"

"Christian, you don't have a choice because if I think some shit is going down that shouldn't be, I'm out. I deserve to be happy and that's all that I will accept. Now, I don't want to talk about this anymore," I said with finality and then I thought of something. "Did you fuck that bitch raw?"

"Hell the fuck NO!" He acted like he was offended. "You know better, girl."

"I thought I knew that you would never cheat on, but boy did you fool me."

"I'm fucking sorry Ivy, now shit," he yelled so loud that he made CJ jump and start crying.

I headed to the kitchen to fix him a bottle. I didn't want to start an argument, but hell, he acted like he had been using the best judgement lately. "Listen, you fucked up and I fucked up, now let's just work through this shit and get past it because I love you and I'm not going *anywhere* and neither are you, so we may as well be happy, right?"

He snatched the bottle away from me and walked out of the kitchen to tell me that the conversation was over.

I would let this shit go for now but this was far from over. We had a lot to talk about and I couldn't wait to get in front of Miss Thing from the bank. She was going to find out why it was important to never mess with my family.

Chapter Fifteen

JERIMIAH

I should have known Keith was on some dirty shit. All of the money he had couldn't have come from being a lawyer. I heard his conversation with the Christian and Messiah guy. So he was selling drugs for them? That's why he got so mad that they didn't like me, because it would mess up their business deals. Well, I was going to make sure that they all went down.

It had been about a month since that day, and I was working with a buddy of mine in the district attorney's office. We went to school together and he owed me one because I got his brother out of some shit a while back. He was kinda lagging more than I wanted him to. He kept giving me the bullshit about having to have a solid case. They had a case against my father-in-law, but they couldn't get anything on those other two bastards.

I tried to get Keri to help me, but lately, she had been on some other shit. I had to slap her a couple nights ago and the bitch had the nerve to hit me back. It took me by surprise for a second because I didn't know what to think about that shit; she had never hit me back before. I couldn't even do anything else. I just got my keys and left. I had been with Bianca ever since.

Bianca was the chick that worked at the Marriot that Christian and Keri used to sneak off to. She was the one who told me just how much of a whore my wife was. Bianca was a really cool chick; she was kinda quiet and she didn't ask for much. She was sexy as hell and could cook her ass off, and her bedroom skills were nothing short of amazing. After I got finish talking to Stephen, the district attorney, then I would be headed back to her house to release some stress.

Come to think of it, I had been gone from the house for damn near a week and not once did Keri call me. She must be up to something. Maybe I should swing by before I head back to Bianca's house. I think I will just do that.

"Mr. Stevens will see you now," his sexy ass receptionist said.

I knew his ass was tapping that. She was too sexy for him not to be. I knew that if it was me, I would be tapping her. I winked at her and she snarled her nose at me. Yep, he was definitely hitting that.

I walked into his little ass office. That was one of the reasons I went into criminal law; that was where the money was. I could fit three of his little ass offices in my big ass office. He had a regular wooded desk and a few pictures of him and his wife, which made me laugh because I knew that he was fucking the receptionist.

"I'm glad to see that this is a joke to you," he said snidely.

"My apologies," I hit him with a smirk.

I was an asshole and I knew it, but that's what made me a damn good lawyer, I didn't care about people's feelings. "I'm just here to make sure that we were still on track with taking these fools down."

"What do you mean 'on track'? We have never been on track." He was looking at me like I had shit on my face. "Like I told you before, we can bring your father-in-law in for questioning, but we don't have shit to hold him on."

"What about the other two?"

"We don't have anything on them either. I have told you that I don't know how many times. If I bring them in now, they will be out within the hour, and then both of our families will be in danger."

"Are you scared of those common criminals?"

He started to laugh. I was starting to get pissed the fuck off. It was like no one wanted to talk about Christian and Messiah. I went to a private investigator and tried to get information on them, and they refused to even work with me after I showed them who I wanted followed, and the same thing happened with the other four PI's I tried to hire.

"You clearly didn't do your research well, because had you done so, you would really let this go."

I looked at him like he was crazy. He had this stupid look

on his face and then it dawned on me, he was on the fucking payroll. That was why he would never do anything about any of this. Not having anything my ass. He wasn't trying to find anything; he had been stringing me along this entire time. If I wanted to get this done, I would have to do it myself.

"Thank you, Stephen, for absolutely nothing."

"If you know what's good for you, you would just let this go and move on. It's not even worth it over a piece of pussy you don't even want."

I just looked at him. We all took an oath to follow the constitutional law, and here I was amongst a bunch of corrupted lawyers.

"How many of you are there?" I nodded in his direction, and he knew just what I was talking about because he smiled.

He must have thought those common thugs could protect him more than the law.

I walked towards the exit of his office and just as I was about to close the door behind me, he spoke.

"There's enough!"

I didn't know what he meant by that, but I didn't like the way it sounded. Instead of responding, I just walked out. As I walked past the receptionist, she looked at me and shook her head. Damn, was she a part of this too? I had to find a way to do this on my own.

Chapter Sixteen

KERI

I danced around my living room, feeling free as a damn bird. Jerimiah hadn't been home in almost a week and I was in heaven. I was so happy not to see him that I didn't know what to do. The last night he was here, he had put his hands on me and I hit his ass back. I was done taking the beatings lying down. Even if he beat my ass, I was going to make sure that he wore one too. That night after that event, something came over me and I didn't know what it was, but I promise it was here to stay. I was tired of being the butt of everyone's joke and they were all going to pay, in one way or another.

Christian and his bullshit had brought out a woman in me that I didn't know existed. The way he just played me like I wasn't there for him when all that shit was going down with him and "his wife". Then to call me a mediocre fuck was a low blow. He took every fuck I had ever given about anyone and threw that shit out the window. Now, I was about to make it my business to make his life a living hell. My first mission was that I was going to show up at Ms. Ivy's house and tell her a little bit about her man. I wasn't sure if she knew about us, but I was going to make sure that she did.

"YOU'RE MY LITTLE SECRET!" I screamed over the music as I continued to drink champagne and dance all over my living room.

"What the fuck are you doing, Keri?" Jerimiah turned down the music and screamed at me. "Are you fucking crazy?"

I laughed. I was a bit tipsy and was not in the mood to see his face. I just wanted him to go back to the bitch that he had been laying up with. I didn't need him here. If he didn't agree to leave, I was going to go. I was on a mission to be happy while ruining everyone else in the process.

"Why are you here?"

"Excuse me?"

"Oh, you heard me." He was shocked by my newfound confidence. His ass had better get used to it because the new Keri was here to stay. "Why the hell are you here? Shouldn't you be laid up with the next bitch? Huh?" I took another sip of my champagne.

"Your ass must me drunk, talking to me like that."

"Nooooooo," I sang. "I'm just tired of your shit, and Daddy's shit, and Christian's shit."

I sobered up really quick then. I didn't mean to let that slip. I didn't want him to know that I had been sleeping with

Christian yet. I was going to use that against him. I wanted to wait until I was in a public place with him to let everyone know that he didn't satisfy his wife so she had to go elsewhere. Shit, my drunk ass messed up everything.

"What does Christian have to do with this?"

"Nothing, I'm drunk."

"Nah, you're bad. Finish what you were saying about Christian."

I didn't say anything. I just walked away and headed to the kitchen to pour another glass of champagne because my buzz was officially gone. I could hear his Stacey Adams clicking behind me. I knew it was about to be some shit.

He grabbed my shoulder, turned me around and slammed me against the counter. I jerked away and he backhanded me. I bent over and held my nose because I could feel the blood about to pour out.

"Don't you ever jerk away from me again. I don't know what the fuck your problem is, but you need to fix that shit and fall in line before your mother has to be burying her fucking daughter."

I raised up and slapped the shit out of him with my bloody hand. I slapped him again and again. I kept swinging and swinging. I was wind milling the hell out of him and I was landing more hits than I was missing. I wanted him to feel everything that I had been feeling lately.

"You stupid bitch!" he screamed before he punched me in the face so hard that I fell.

My head hit the ground and everything faded to black.

I woke up to beeping noises. I couldn't open my left eye, but I could open my right eye a little. When I did, the light was so bright that I had to shut them immediately.

"Honey, are you awake? I'm so glad you're okay," I heard my mom say. "Who did this to you?"

As bad as I wanted to make Jerimiah pay for what he did to me, I had more pressing issues that I wanted to address.

"Who did this to you, baby?" my mom asked again.

"Christian, Christian Hope."

Chapter Seventeen

IVY

I was still going back and forth about Christian and I in my heart. I needed to talk to someone who would just listen and not give me advice that they thought would be beneficial. My girls listened, but they always gave unwarranted advice. I needed a man's point of view. I needed to talk to my daddy, Big Stew.

I knew that he was still on vacation. He said that he needed time away from everything for a little while, so that he could have some peace and let go of everything that happened with Ma Stew and Junior. He told us to call him if he needed anything, but I knew he didn't have time for all of my issues, even though I really needed his advice.

I picked up the phone, called him and he answered on the first ring.

"Hey, baby girl, how are you?"

This was the happiest I had ever heard him since Ma died.

"I'm okay, Daddy, why are you so chipper?"

"I'm not chipper, baby, I'm just at peace. And I'm excited to hear from you. How have you been?"

I immediately started sobbing. I didn't want Daddy to hate Christian, but I needed him to give my advice.

"What is wrong with you, Ivy?" His voice was stern and filled with concern.

"Christian is cheating on me," I cried into the phone and he was silent.

I didn't know what to think. I didn't want him and Christian to go to war, but I needed to know what to do.

"Baby girl, don't cry. Sometimes men do dumb shit and it's not because we don't love you, it's because we don't know how to take certain things. Does that make sense?"

"So it's okay for him to cheat because he is too stubborn to swallow his fucking pride?"

"You better watch your damn mouth little girl, you ain't too old for me to get in your shit. You know I don't play that disrespectful shit."

I had to calm myself down because he didn't have a problem coming from wherever the hell he was to whoop my ass and then go back. I swallowed hard and got my emotions under control really quick.

"I'm sorry, sir, I just don't want you making excuses for him because you look at him like your son," I said a few octaves lower than how I started off.

"Better!" he said then took a deep breath. "I'm about to

hit you with some real shit, baby girl. That abortion you had crushed that man. That shit had him questioning his manhood. He felt like you didn't think he was worthy enough to protect you and his family. He second guessed his position in your life and yours in his. Was he wrong? Yes, 100%, but so were you, sweetheart. In our line of work, loyalty is everything and when you went behind his back and did what you did, he considered that disloyal. That's where his doubt kicked. in Do I think he should have used that as a means to be unfaithful? No, but he's human, and people make mistakes. It's up to you whether or not you want to forgive him, but if you choose to forgive him, you can't continue to throw this in his face, okay?"

"He throws the abortion in my face all the time."

"Then he has not fully forgiven you yet, and that's a conversation that the two of you need to sit down and have."

"Yes, sir," I said in a defeated tone because he wasn't telling me what I wanted to hear. "Daddy?"

"Yes, baby?"

"Did you ever cheat on Ma?"

"I hate to have to say this, but yes, I did, and it was the worst mistake of my life. But again, I'm human and humans make mistakes. She chose to forgive me, and that made us stronger."

"Okay, I get it," I said sadly.

"If you don't want to forgive him, you don't have to, but just make sure you are prepared to live without him, because no man is going to live with constant reminders of his mistakes. If you know you are not going to be able to fully forgive, do him and yourself a favor and leave."

"I know; I'm going to have to sleep on it."

"I didn't tell you what you wanted to hear, did I?" he laughed.

"Not at all."

"I always want you girls to be able to handle your own and make your own decisions. From the moment you came to stay with us, I taught you to always stand strong in what you believe. If you believe that this was not a mistake and that he will keep doing it, then let it go, baby. In the end, it's all about your happiness. But I know you love that man and he loves you, so if y'all work together and communicate, things will be okay." That's why I loved him, he was so real. "Now, I can have a little talk with my son-in-law if you want me to. I'll even kick his ass for you. What good would that do though, if you are going to be right back together?"

"You're right!"

"Just remember though, one time is a mistake, two times is a choice. So if he does that shit again, shoot him in the kneecaps."

I laughed so hard because I knew that he would make me feel better with all of this. That's why I loved Daddy. He always made everything all better. I just hoped that he was right about us being able to work it out. I didn't want to see myself without Christian, but I wouldn't play the fool for him either. I guess we would see how everything went.

"Alright, princess. I am going to hit the beach and enjoy this sunset."

"Okay, Daddy. Have fun and enjoy yourself. I will see you when you get back."

"I love you, baby girl."

"I love you too, Daddy."

Chapter Eighteen

CHRISTIAN

"Nigga, you ready for this shit I'm about to lay on you?" Raheem said.

My niggas had made the move to North Carolina and I was happy to have them here. They never missed a damn beat and had been working their asses off. Business had definitely picked up for them.

"What's up, nigga? You know I don't like that trivia shit."

"That nigga y'all had me look into, Keith Russell, that lawyer nigga?" I shook my head and took a swig of my beer.

We were currently chilling in Messiah's basement. The women were upstairs but we came down here to discuss some business. "He has been working with a new connect. Business ain't slow down, that shit is booming. He was trying to cut y'all out."

"Oh word?" Messiah said with that damn smirk on his face. "Who is the connect?

"Some nigga that hired us to kill him," Shaheed chimed in.

Ain't this some shit. He trying to undercut us, and unknowingly, he had the nigga he was putting his trust in trying to murk his dumb ass. That was exactly why it didn't pay to be disloyal. That shit always backfired.

"The nigga probably wanted to take over the territory. When I was scoping that nigga's shit, I got to peep his territory, and it's nice. They make a lot of money over there," Raheem said.

"Hmmmmmmm, what kinda shit that nigga serving out there? Is it better than what we got?"

"Nah, from what I hear, it's some weak shit."

Raheem shook his head and laughed because he knew where I was going with this.

"We need to hook up with him and find out where he's getting his shit from. We might be able to step in and help out." I rubbed my hands together.

"Let us take care of the problem first, nigga."

"We know that, nigga," Messiah spoke up.

We chopped it up for a minute. It had been a minute since we all had got together like this. We all had kids now, and the twins and their wives had been working like crazy. Plus, Messiah and I were trying to get this club going; time had been real stingy lately.

Messiah started telling us about the club and his visions for how shit would be. He got it set up where we wouldn't have to be there all the time. We were going to hire staff to make sure all that shit was done. The twins were gone put a state-of-the-art security system in the building so we didn't have to worry about nobody stealing shit. Messiah came up with a fool-proof system that would make it damn near impossible to steal from us.

He told me that that was Reign's biggest issue, that the club would take him away from them, so he came up with a way that it wouldn't. I was grateful for that because I was already in hot water with Ivy, and I needed to take every minute that I could to make her realize that I was everything that she thought I was.

"Ivy hasn't shot you yet, nigga?" Shamaad just had to start with that shit.

"Shut the fuck up, 'Maad."

"No, nigga, you shut up. I almost fucked Jess's white ass up because of you."

Shamaad was serious as fuck. I wanted to laugh, but he looked like he had some real shit to say so I was gone let him get it out. "Questioning me and shit. Did you know he was cheating?" He put his hands on his hip and started rolling his neck around and speaking in a high-pitched voice. "Was yo' ass cheating too? Huh? Was you, Shamaad? What was y'all doing why he was cheating Shamaad, huh? Answer me? What were you doing, huh?"

We were all doubled over in laughter. I couldn't fucking breathe. He had his hand pointed just like Jess does when she was fussing at his ass, and he was so serious.

"I bet not find out you was doing shit or I'ma shoot your black ass, you hear me?" He bent over like he was getting in someone's face. "I had to rape her white ass that day."

"What the fuck are you talking about, nigga?" Messiah asked between laughter.

"She wouldn't shut the fuck up so I slammed her head in the couch and fucked her until he went to sleep, and then I left her ass there, butt ass naked, ass up and everything."

This nigga was a fool. I felt so bad for Jess sometimes, but she was low key just as fucking crazy as him. After I finally got myself together, I heard the doorbell ring. I wonder who the fuck it was because it was pushing six at night and everyone that knew where I lived was already here. So who the fuck was at my door?

I ran upstairs with everyone on my heels. When I got to the front, I could hear Ivy arguing with someone and it sounded like a man.

"Who the fuck is at my door?"

"Mr. Hope? Are you Mr. Christian Hope?"

I noticed that it was the fucking police. I hadn't done shit, so I wanted to know what the fuck they wanted. "Sir, we need you to go down to the station with us."

"The fuck for? I ain't did shit!"

"Hell no, Christian, don't go. It's a setup, they gon' shoot yo ass!" Shamaad yelled out.

"Shut up, Shamaad!" everyone yelled out in unison.

"Aight, when something happens to his black ass, then what?"

Shamaad's ass was always joking around.

"What am I being charged with?"

"For the assault of Keri Straggs."

I looked at the officer, waiting on him to say sike because every one of them that were there was on my payroll. That's why they were being cool as shit and not trying no funny shit. The one that was in the front mouthed, "I'll fix this."

I just shook my head and turned to look at Ivy and she was pissed the fuck off. Great! Now she was going to think that I was near that bitch again, and that was the furthest thing from the case.

"We are taking him down to the station. If you have an alibi for the night of September 3rd, we can get this cleared up right now," the officer standing in front of me stated.

His ass was scared, they all were. They knew the consequences of us not being safe from shit like that.

"Did you say September 3rd?" Ivy asked.

"Yes, ma'am."

"As in two days ago?"

Again, the officer nodded.

She was starting to see that this shit was a setup because we went out to dinner that night and chilled after. I was going to kill Keri; I couldn't wait to get my hands on that bitch. "We went to dinner at Jeffery's, we had reservations and everything. You can call them and I can get you the receipt where he paid."

That was my baby, bossing up on people. She gave me the head nod, but I could tell that this shit was far from over.

Even though she knew I hadn't been near that bitch, my actions are causing all of this turmoil right now. I was going to have to dig deep in my bag of tricks to make this up to her.

The officers cuffed me and took me to the car. I didn't bother saying shit, I just let them do their thing. Ivy was calling the lawyer by the time I walked out of the house. I wasn't worried, because by the time I was done, there would be no case and I damn sure wouldn't make it past the holding cell.

During the entire ride to the police station, I thought of every way that I could kill Keri. I couldn't believe that she had gone through these lengths. She told me that she was married and she wasn't trying to leave her marriage, which was the one reason I continued to fuck with her after that first time. I shouldn't have been fucking with her at all, but I had a lapse in judgement. That shit wouldn't happen again, with anybody.

We got to the station; they did all that processing shit and about two hours later, I was walking out of the precinct. Ivy was standing there, looking pissed. I looked around hoping that someone came with her, but she was alone. I knew she was about to tear me a new one, so I took a deep breath and got ready for the heat.

"How long were you fucking her?"

"We already talked about this, Ivy. I told you it was only about two weeks."

"Two weeks, and this bitch is acting like this? Making up fake police reports and shit? Somebody beat her ass real good though. It doesn't have shit on what the hell I'm going to do to her."

"I'll handle it, Ivy. I don't want you to get mixed up in my shit."

"Haven't you handled enough?"

"Come on now, don't do that."

"Don't do what? I didn't do shit, you did. And now look, Christian. We got the muthafuckin police showing up on our doorstep for some dumb shit. You know what I do for a living? I can't afford for your dick to get us into some shit that we can't get out of."

"Are you going to bring this shit up every time we fight?"

She didn't say anything and that pissed me off. With the abortion, she told me that if I was going to keep bringing it up then we were going to have to go our separate ways.

"Did you hear me, Ivy?"

She still said nothing. She just stared at the road and dipped in and out of traffic.

"DID YOU HEAR WHAT THE FUCK I SAID?" I yelled so loud that it made her jump.

I was tired of playing these little games. She thought that she could say what the fuck she wanted to say to me and I was supposed to just lay back and take it. Yes, I fucked up, but I would not sit and let her tear me down for the one mistake I made, when I was not allowed to bring up the shit she did.

"YES!" she yelled back.

"Are we or are we not gon' talk about this shit every time we fight?"

"No, but this time it's necessary because that bullshit is the reason why I had to bail your ass out of jail. So, like I said, I will be taking care of this bum bitch, and you are to stay the hell away from her."

"You gon' make me fuck you up, Ivy, that's what the fuck gon' happen."

That was all I could think of to say at that moment because she had a good point. I still didn't want her getting into any shit, so I would call the twins and get the girls on it. They could do it quick and their emotions wouldn't be involved. When emotions got involved that was when shit went wrong, and I was not trying to risk that shit.

Chapter Nineteen

KEITH

I was meeting with Christian and Messiah today to re-up. They still weren't trying to let me cut back on my amount. So right now, I was paying double for all my product because I had also made a commitment with Snake to get just as much from him.

I just knew that Messiah and Christian would budge, but I was wrong. I was going to try one more time to get them to come down. If not, I was going to have to take some extreme measures.

My new connect's prices were lower in cost, but the quality of the product wasn't as good as what I was getting from Christian and Messiah. With the amount I could get from the new supplier at the cost he was giving me, it would make my profit almost triple. I would take what little I got from Christian and Messiah and mix it with the weak shit, and have an okay batch. My plan was foolproof, now I just needed a way to get these muthafuckas on board.

Right as I was about to walk out of the house, my phone rang and it was my buddy, District Attorney Stephen Stevens. He was my eyes and ears on the inside. I wondered what he wanted. He was the one who introduced me to Christian and Messiah, and from the moment he did, I had been making money. But unfortunately, there was a better deal on the table.

"Talk to me, young buck," I called him by the nickname I had for him.

"I see you have made a little enemy, old man," he said in a hushed voice.

He was calling me from his cell phone so I wondered why he was whispering.

"What you talking about, Stephen?"

"Your son-in-law came to my office demanding that I help him take you, Christian, and Messiah down. He was mad about one of them sleeping with Keri, but he hates her, so I don't understand why he's running around here playing with fire for someone he doesn't even care about."

I was still stuck on the fact that he said that Jerimiah came to him about setting me up. How in the hell did he even know that I was doing anything other than getting drug dealers off? I had to think long and hard. I was always careful not to say the wrong thing to him or anything like that.

The only other time that he could have heard something was... Shit! At the event. When I was done talking to Christian and Messiah, he popped up out of nowhere asking if I was okay. I was so sure that he hadn't heard anything, but I could've been wrong. He had been acting weird ever since, avoiding me at the office, and barely making eye contact with me. I should have known he wouldn't be about this life. My plan was going to be to expand and have him be a part of it.

His ass took that oath a little too serious for me. I used to until I saw the many ways the system could fuck you up, and my whole mind frame changed.

"You hear what I said, Keith?"

I had zoned the fuck out and I barely heard anything he said. I heard the important shit and that was that Jerimiah had to go. I doubt my daughter would be sad at all. She would probably dance at his damn funeral.

"Yeah, I heard you. I will take care of it."

"Be careful, and let me know if you need me."

"'Preciate that!"

I hung up the phone with him and headed out the door to go meet Christian and Messiah. I would use that as leverage for them to lighten my load a bit.

Once I pulled up to their warehouse, I grabbed my briefcase and got out. I always carried my briefcase just in case someone saw me. They would just think that I was going to see a client. I couldn't risk them seeing me with people like Christian and Messiah, which would surely raise suspicions.

"Keith, you're late my man," that cocky ass Messiah said as soon as I walked in to the warehouse.

If I could choose to only work with Christian, I would, because that Messiah scared the shit out of me.

"Well, I was late because I got a call from District Attorney Stevens. He told me that we have an enemy lurking around and asking questions."

They both just looked at me and didn't say anything. I didn't know if they were waiting on me to finish or they were processing what I was saying. The look on Messiah's face let me know to continue with what I needed to say. I swear that muthafucka was so damn impatient.

"Jerimiah, my son-in-law, is trying to take us down. He's mad because you fucked his wife," I said, pointing to Christian.

"Oh yeah," Messiah said and then walked off toward the back of the building.

"Where the hell is he going?"

"That's none of your got damn business. You got the money?"

"Look, I was thinking since I looked out for y'all, you would cut me some slack and let me drop my shipment back down. You know, as a show of appreciation," I chuckled to lighten the atmosphere that had just gotten tense.

"Maybe you should stop thinking then 'cause you ain't told us shit. You know like I know everyone in the precinct works for us, so whether you told us or not, we would have found out."

"But—"

"But nothing, I'm tired of hearing your fucking whining. You made the got damn commitment and now you say that you can't fulfill it. Why is that, Keith?"

I could tell that he was getting aggravated because his demeanor was cold. "From what I hear, you're doing great out that way. I had a few guys go check it out and I hear you bringing in way more than you are getting from us. You wouldn't be trying to short cut us, now would you, Keith?"

"No, no, I would never do that."

"So, how is it that you are pushing way more than you are getting from us? You watering our shit down?"

"No, that's not it at all. I don't know where you are getting your information from, but they are wrong. I would never do anything to cross y'all."

I knew I was fucked. I wondered which one of my guys were talking because if there was a new face hanging around, I would have known about it. I needed to get to the bottom of it because I could not afford to have them as an enemy. "I will get all of this straightened out, here's your money."

I handed him the briefcase and I headed for the door.

I could hear Messiah coming back into the room where we were. He didn't say anything, but when I looked back, he was staring at me with the evilest look I had ever seen. I hurried my ass right on out of there and didn't look back. I left my briefcase and all. They could keep that shit for all I cared. I had to get my shit under control before I ended up dead.

Chapter Twenty

CHRISTIAN

Ivy's ass was giving me the cold shoulder like a muthafucka. If it didn't have anything to do with CJ, she wasn't trying to hear that shit. She was starting to piss me off, but I was trying to give her some space because I know it was a lot to deal with. I couldn't believe Keri did that bullshit. I should've known her ass would be on some shit though, by the way she acted at that party.

I was on my way now to pick up Shamaad and Messiah so we could go get all of our money out of the bank she worked at. Ivy made it perfectly clear that I was to have no dealings with her at all, even if it was about my money. So, I thought it was best to go withdraw my money and just start over with another bank.

I pulled up to Shamaad's house and I could hear arguing, so I rolled down my window because I wanted to be nosey.

"Shamaad, I'ma fuck you up. You did that shit on purpose. If I pop up pregnant, I'm leaving you."

Jess was mad as hell.

"Shut yo' white ass up, you ain't going nowhere but in there and fix my kids something to eat. Ill hog tie yo' ass to a kitchen chair and force feed you this nut, now keep on."

"I swear I hate you sometimes."

"Yeah, but you love this sweet meat," he laughed and jumped in the car, as Jess hurled her shoe at my truck.

"Yo, if she scratches my shit, you're paying for it," I warned him, and of course he just laughed.

"Jess on some dumb shit, talking about me using condoms and shit." His face turned serious. "I told her ass no and she went out and bought them shits anyway."

"What the fuck you do, man?" I couldn't wait to hear what the fuck his ignorant ass done did to this girl for her to be cussing him and hurling shoes at my damn car.

"I opened every last one of them and cut the tops off. I needs to feel the gushy," he smirked and moved his pointer finger and middle finger in the scissor motion. "So this morning while the twins were sleep, I went to work on her ass. She wasn't even paying attention when I put the mutha-fucka on, so I went on about my business. When we were done, I laid on the bed beside her and she sat up and thought the condom broke." All I could do was shake my head. "She got all worried but I started playing in that puss and she forgot all about it. Then she got up to grab another condom and realized that I had cut them bitches up. Her white ass turned beet red."

This nigga was in the passenger seat laughing his ass off.

"She gon' mess around and cut yo' dumb ass."

"Jessica ain't gon' do shit but what she been doing."

Hell, at this point, I would wear a condom just to get some pussy. I ain't had none since she had the baby.

"Her simple ass should have known I wasn't about to wear no damn condom. She better go get some birth control and not that five year shit either. I'm giving her ass two years to recover from the twins and then I'm loading her up again."

"What if she don't want any more kids?" I asked as we pulled in Messiah's driveway and he jogged out with a pissed off Reign in the doorway. What the fuck was going on this morning? "What the fuck you do?"

"I'm going with your ass nigga," he mugged me through the rearview mirror. "Ivy done called her starting shit. I told yo' monkey ass if this shit boils over into my household that I was going to whoop yo' ass, didn't I?"

"Shut the fuck up, ain't nobody wanting to hear that shit. Let's go get this over with before Ivy start blowing my phone the fuck up."

"That's yo' got damn fault! We told you not to do that dumb shit, but did you listen to us?"

"Fuck y'all!" I was tired of hearing the 'I told you so's'.

"Nah nigga, I'm good. I released enough of my kids this morning," Shamaad's ignorant ass chimed in.

We ignored him and continued to the bank. I hoped like

hell that she was at work because I planned on showing my fucking ass right after I got all my money out of there.

The ride to the bank was filled with talks about getting up with that Snake nigga. Raheem and Shaheed were waiting on the other half of the money before they could take care of Keith. We were trying to wait that shit out, but we needed to act soon.

We pulled up to the bank and got out. As soon as I walked in, I saw the bitch sitting there grinning in some nigga's face. When we got close enough, I noticed that it was Ivy's ex Ty that she was talking to.

My blood started to boil immediately. I wanted to shoot that muthafucka so bad, but there was no way I would be able to clean this shit up with all of these witnesses. I just looked at him and nodded my head. I now knew exactly where those pictures came from.

Keri's eyes caught mine and every ounce of color drained out of her face. You would have thought she saw a ghost or something. Somebody really did a number to her face, but it damn sure wasn't me. The fact that she was sitting there in front of Ivy's ex had me wanting to do way more.

"Mr. Hope, hi, my name is Shantel, and I will be helping you with your withdrawal. We are really hoping that you would reconsider," the manager of the bank said as she was walking us to her office.

"The only way that I would consider leaving my money in here is if that bitch is fired," I said, pointing to Keri, who was looking in my direction.

"That's a bitch move, Chris," Shamaad said, causing all of us to laugh.

"Fuck you, 'Maad, that bitch gon' learn today!"

"I'm sorry, sir, I cannot just fire someone without just cause."

"She's fucking her clients, is that enough?"

"Excuse me, sir?"

She acted like she was taken aback by what I said, but her eyes were telling a totally different story as they bounced between the three of us, and her body language was asking for one of us to take her in that back room and kill that pussy. Too bad I wasn't going that fucking route again.

"You heard the man, that bitch been sucking the gristle off his dick!" Shamaad said, loud enough for the whole room to hear him. He started dancing and singing, "He was balls deep, I said balls deep."

Why in the fuck did I bring him again?

Keri jumped up out of her seat, clearly embarrassed because Shamaad had the whole room either shocked as hell or doubled over in laughter. She ran over to where we were standing, outside of the manager's office.

She jumped in my face and slapped the piss out of me.

I grabbed her hand, shoved it behind her back and got real close to her ear, "You are going to wish you never did that."

She snatched her hands back and backed away like she was scared, as she should be, because she was definitely going to be taking a dirt nap for that little stunt she had just pulled.

"KERI, IN MY OFFICE, NOW!"

"Yeah, Keri, in the fucking office, NOW!" Shamaad mocked.

She turned and looked at him like she wanted to hit him too.

"Bitch, I will skin yo' ugly ass alive."

I could have sworn that I saw the bank manager smile but I could have been wrong.

"I'm so sorry, gentlemen. Can we please reschedule while I take care of this?"

"Yeah, just call me and we will set up a time to meet again. I can tell you now that if she is leaving, then there is no need to call because my money can just stay here."

She didn't answer, she just shook her head. That bank did not want to lose out on the money that we had in there. Hell, our money alone could keep this bank open. They would be stupid to lose us as clients.

We hopped back in the car and once we were all in, I turned to look at Shamaad and burst out laughing.

"Dude, what the fuck is wrong with you?"

"What the fuck I do?" he asked with a smirk on his face.

"Balls deep, nigga? You really made a damn song about that shit?"

"Sure the fuck did. I'm 'bout to put that on a mixtape!"

"Nigga!" Messiah and I said at the same time.

Chapter Twenty-One

MESSIAH

fter we left the bank, we wanted to head over to the club to check its progress. I texted Reign and told her that was where we would be if they wanted to come over. She asked me how long we would be over there and I told her for a while. She said that they would stop by after Ivy's last appointment.

I was so proud of us. Yes, we still did our thing in the streets, but we were about to be the owners of the biggest club that Charlotte had ever seen. The layout of the club was amazing and I couldn't wait until the doors opened.

"Can you believe this shit will be opened in a few more weeks?" Christian beamed.

"I can't fucking wait!" I damn near yelled.

"Too bad we're all damn near married because the hoes would be in abundance," Shamaad's dumb ass said.

"Where the fuck has Supreme been at?"

"His ass is still the fucking same. Ain't ready to grow up. He shot some nigga over Angel's ass the other day, and then went out and cheated on her the same got damn night. She left his ass, but she will be right back with him."

"That got damn Supreme."

My little brother reminded me of me at that age—I just didn't give a fuck. Only difference was that I didn't have anybody that I cared about. I just pretty much did me and didn't give a fuck abut anybody's feelings. Supreme, on the other hand had Angel, who was Reign's cousin. He loved that girl, he was just scared to get hurt, and by letting go of his feelings, it would leave an opening for him to get hurt. I told him just like I told Christian's ass that if he didn't get his shit together, he was going to end up by himself.

"The nigga acts like yo' hoe ass," I told Christian.

"Yo, fuck you, nigga." We all laughed, thinking back to the day I had to whoop his ass in the boxing ring. "Maybe you need to have a one on one with him in the ring."

"That doesn't sound like a bad idea. He always did think he could whoop my ass."

We talked and laughed a little bit more at my brother's expense. When we got to the building, I almost wanted to squeal like a little bitch, but I held that shit in because I would never hear the end of it.

I wanted the girls to do all the decorating, so I hired one of the best interior decorators on this side of the world to come up and hook us up. That's why we wanted the girls here.

The inside of the building was nice as fuck. The bars and the countertops were black marble. I wanted the place to have an elegant yet sexy feel to it, and nothing said sexy like black. The walls were painted a deep burgundy and there were mirrors everywhere. The dance floor on the bottom floor was one big ass mirror.

"Oh my goodness this is amazing," Reign said as she walked in the club. "You really did it, baby."

"I love this," Ivy said, looking around.

"I thought y'all were waiting and coming later."

"My last appointment canceled so we wanted to come and surprise you."

Christian walked over and hugged Ivy from behind, and for once, she let him. She laid her head back on his chest and he kissed her on the forehead. That was how it was supposed to be; we were all supposed to be happy and living like one big ass happy family. For once, everyone looked content. Of course, that shit wouldn't last long.

"I guess I'm late to the party," Keri said as she walked in with one of her flunkies.

"You literally got two point six seconds to make your way out of this fucking club or I'm going to make you wish you never met him."

She was too calm; Ivy was one to always show her emotions. Her and Reign would flip in a matter of seconds but the fact that she was calm at the moment was odd.

"Get the fuck out, Keri," was all that Christian said.

"No! You got me fired and somebody is about to pay for this shit."

This bitch was making me mad because she was in here showing her ass and the interior decorator had just walked through the door. I paid a lot of money to get her to come here.

"You're so worried about your precious bit—" was the only thing that she got out of her mouth before Ivy let loose on her ass.

I had never seen Ivy fight like that before; she was giving that girl everything she had. The look in Ivy's eyes was scary. She wanted to make sure that Keri felt everything that she had been feeling.

"Somebody get her off of her, she's gonna kill her!" The friend was standing there like she wanted to jump in. "Fine, I'll break it up."

She stuck her hand in like she was going to touch Ivy and Reign two pieced her ass. She had her laid out.

The interior decorator lady went on about her business like they weren't fighting like hell down there.

"Didn't - I - tell - yo - ass - to - get the fuck out of here!" Ivy hit her with every word she said.

"Fuck you, bitch."

"No bitch, fuck you," I don't even know where Ivy had her gun, but she came up with that muthafucka and had it pointed at that bitch's head. "Talk that shit now."

"Please, no, please. I'm sorry, I'll leave."

"I bet you will."

Ivy brought the gun down on her face and something broke because you could hear the bones pop. Ivy got off of her and Keri couldn't do anything but roll around on the ground in agony. Too bad Ivy's ass wasn't through with her yet. She grabbed her by her hair and dragged her to the exit and slung her out the door. "The next time I tell your ass to get the fuck out, bitch, you do so. And stay the fuck away from my family."

"You fucking crazy ass nut, you worse than Rambo over there," Shamaad shook his head while pointing at Reign.

She flipped him off while she went and got the friend by the hair to drag her out.

"You good, sis?" Reign hugged Ivy.

I loved their bond; they are just as close as Messiah and I.

"You whooped that bitch's ass."

"I feel better," she smiled. "Do you see what happens when you stray?"

"Yes, ma'am. I swear on everything I love that that shit won't happen again."

"Fuck no, or we hitting that ring again!"

We started laughing and the girls looked around because they didn't know what I was talking about. They didn't need to know; as long as Christian knew, we were good.

Chapter Twenty-Two

KERI

"Why in the hell did you bring me into this mess?" Sherrie had the nerve to ask.

"Bring you in to it? Mrs. I'm your rider, these bitches don't want none, but I dragged you into this? I'm confused."

I looked at the bitch like she had sprouted three heads. Not once did I ask her to come with me to handle this. She worked at the bank with me and saw what went down, and she was the one talking about 'let's go find him and show him that we don't play that'. Now that we both got fucked up, she wanted to talk about why I brought her there.

"Well you clearly didn't tell me what kind of people we were dealing with. Those heffas were like real life MMA fighters or something."

We had just got back from the hospital from getting my broken nose tended to. She broke my nose in three places; I didn't even know that was possible. They damn near had to reconstruct my nose. Sherrie had a few bruised ribs, amongst other things.

I needed to call my daddy and let him know what had just happened. I needed him to contact one of his friends that he "worked" with to handle Christian and Rhonda Rousey.

"What do you want, Keri? I'm busy," he picked up and said immediately. No hey honey, nothing. I knew he hated me, but dang, the least he could do was pretend.

"I need your help; I was just attacked by Christian and his Pitbull."

"Not this shit again. I'm still paying from the last time you got him arrested. Leave that man alone. He does not want you, and with good reason. You can't even keep your own man happy, and you think that you can take someone else's? Get a life, Keri, and leave that man alone before you get us all killed."

He was aggravated with me, and yes, I lied before, but I wasn't lying now. They did attack me, well she did. I just needed him on my side for once.

"Are we clear, Keri, because the next time you do something to that man and he threatens your life, I'm not saving you, do you understand?"

Did he really just say that he would let someone kill me? What kind of father was he? I bet he didn't know that I knew all about his little illegal bullshit. I wondered what he would do if I told the world that he was a dirty lawyer who sold drugs on the side? Maybe I would just do that.

Instead of answering him, I just hung up the phone. I was literally out here by myself. I had no one but my mother. Sherrie showed me today that she was not a real friend so I damn sure couldn't count on her.

Ty! That was who I could call. I snatched up my phone and hit him up.

"Yes, Keri," he said like I was bothering him.

"Who pissed in your Cheerios?"

"What do you want?"

"Come to my house, I just got attacked."

"And what does that have to do with me?"

"Your little bitch did it." I said that, then hung up the phone before he started his rant about me not calling Ivy a bitch.

I knew that he would be here because he was going to want to know why I was around Ivy for her to attack me. I didn't know what the big deal about this bitch was, but she had every one graveling at her feet and I didn't understand.

I told Sherrie that she had to go and escorted her out. I went upstairs and took a shower and attempted to put some makeup over all of the bruises that were on my face. I put on a cute little nighty. I needed to be cute for what I was about to ask Ty to do for me. Maybe I could get laid in the process.

An hour passed and he still wasn't there. I was on my third glass of wine and was about to call him until I heard a knock on the door. When I opened the door, I stood there with my hands on my hips, in the sexiest pose that I could muster up.

He looked me up and down, that made me blush a little,

thinking that he liked what he saw. When his eyes reached my face again, he laughed and he slid right by me into the house.

"What's so funny?"

"You."

"What about this is funny?" I twirled around and struck another pose.

"You. What do you call yourself doing, seducing me? You didn't have to go through all of that. If you wanted to be fucked, then that's all you had to say. But that's about all I can do for you!"

He walked back towards the door.

"No!" I screamed out desperately. "I need you!"

"You need me for what? There is nothing that I can do for you, Keri."

"I need you to kill Christian," I blurted out.

"Do you know what you are asking me to do?"

"Yes, but the only way that you will ever get Ivy is if he's dead."

"Do you know how hard it will be to kill that man, and do you know if I did, how many people will be after me?"

"But you want Ivy, right?"

"Yes, but if I can get Ivy to love me again, then we will be together."

It was my turn to laugh. "If she didn't leave him after the photos, nothing will work."

"Why do you want this man dead so bad?"

"Because he hurt me. I want every man that has ever hurt me to suffer."

"I don't want to be part of your little game, Keri. I just want Ivy."

"And if you kill Christian, you will have Ivy. If we're smart about it, we won't get caught."

"You gotta let me think on this, this is a lot," he said and then walked to the door.

"Wait! One more thing."

"What?"

I walked over to where he was standing by the door. I pushed his back towards the door and unzipped his pants. He grabbed my hands and pushed me back.

"Please," I felt like I needed to convince him that this was the right thing to do. Maybe if I gave him a little pussy, he would see things my way and agree to help me. "Fuck me!"

He pushed me back over towards the couch and told me to take off my nighty.

I lifted my nighty over my head and threw it across the couch. I slipped out of my thong that was now drenched.

He moved over to where I was and pulled down his pants. He had the smoothest caramel colored rod that I ever seen. The hook that he had in it made me want to swallow him whole, but he didn't give me a chance. He threw me back on the couch, got down on his knees and pulled me to the edge. He entered me with so much force that I thought he would split me in two.

The curve in his dick started hitting places that no one had ever been. My body shuddered every time he slid out and back in. He took his hand and started to play with my hardened nipples and I swear I came off his touch alone.

"How did she ever leave you for him?"

He stopped moving and looked down at me. I couldn't quite read his expression, I just hoped he wasn't done because I wanted to finish out this ride. I had never felt anything like it.

"You really mean that?"

"Huh?"

"I'm better than him?"

Was he serious? If his dick wasn't so good, I would curse him out and tell him to leave. At a time like this, he was worried about Christian's bedroom game? Men and their fucking egos.

"Yes, you're better, now fuck me."

I guess that gave him the mojo that he needed. He threw my legs across his shoulders and started moving his hips in a circular motion. His thumb was attacking my clit and I was about to explode.

"This feels so good, ohhhhhh, I'm about to cum."

He didn't talk back, he just sped up his motions and spread my legs. He reached behind my back and sat me up. When his lips touched mine, I thought that I was going to melt. I got my cowgirl on and started riding the hell out of him while he held me in the air by my legs.

"Do that shit girl," he moaned out.

"Yesssss, just like that, I want to ride."

He stood up with me still in his arms and his dick still

inside me, and sat down on the couch with me on top of him. His hands gripped my ass, urging me to move. I started moving my hips in a circular motion, real nice and slow. His thumb and my clit had become friends because they were joined together.

I rose to the top of his dick and just bounced on the head of it like I was jumping on a pogo stick. He threw his head back in pleasure, and that shit fueled my ego because then I started bouncing what little ass I did have up and down on his pole. I was in heaven.

Right as I was about to cum, the front door swung open. My eyes got big and I just knew it was about to be some shit. I was starting to dismount my position until the little bitch from the hotel popped her head in the door.

"What the hell is going on here?" Jerimiah asked, but I just ignored him and started moving on Ty again.

Ty grabbed my waist and attempted to move me off him, but I grinded further down on him and that took all the fight away from him.

"Keri."

I was almost there, I just needed him to shut up for a few more minutes.

"When ummmmm, I'm do—sssssssssssss done we can talk, ohhhh shit!"

I threw my head back to add theatrics. He looked back at Jerimiah, who was looking at me in both amazement and shock. He attempted to get up again and I gave him the death stare. He got the hint and just relaxed against the couch. I knew I was going to get my ass whooped for this so I figured I may as well get me a nut out of it.

Ty grabbed my waist. I thought he was about to stop me again, but instead, he started guiding my hips, and I leaned down and kissed him. I threw my hair over my shoulder and went on the ride of my life. I couldn't believe that Jerimiah was just standing there letting this go on. I guess he was shocked, or he was just a pussy that beat women and was scared of a man.

"Fuck, I'm about to cum," Ty moaned out as he gripped my hair.

"Ooooohhhhhhhh, ummmm, hmmmmmm." He held my waist up and began thrusting upward. My titties were bouncing all out of control. "Shhhhiitiittttttttt!"

I felt myself being lifted off of Ty and thrown to the floor. I guess he snapped out of his state of shock. I was mad as hell because I was almost there.

Ty's bitch ass jumped up and grabbed his shit and hit the door. He didn't even wait around to see if I was going to be okay. He just got his shit and hit the door. Fuck, he probably wouldn't help me now.

"Bianca, take my car and go to your house."

"But why aren't you coming?"

"Don't ask me any questions, just go."

"No, you need to come with me right now. I'm not leaving unless you are coming with me."

He moved in close to me. "Go upstairs and don't come

down until I tell you to, and I mean it. I'm going to take her home and then we have some things to talk about."

I didn't say anything and I didn't move either. As soon as he was out of this house, I was too. He must have thought that I was crazy. I was not about to sit around here and let him beat my ass.

He grabbed her by her arm and escorted her out.

I went right upstairs and packed me a bag. The mutha-fucka took my car keys but not the keys to his Bentley. I guess I would be running in style.

Things had been going better between Christian and me lately. We had actually been getting along. I wouldn't sit here and say that shit was perfect because it wasn't; we still had a long way to go, but we were making progress. I still had doubts every time he left the house after we argued. I always thought that he was going to do the shit that he did before. I was working on that within myself, but it was hard as hell when that was my life just a few short months ago.

Plus, we still hadn't had sex yet. I wasn't ready and he seemed to understand that and never pressured me. We came real close a few times, but all I could think about was him slinging that good dick in another bitch and that just ruined it all for me.

I was now sitting at work looking through old pictures of

me and Christian. I swear I missed my man. I needed to get the crazy thoughts out of my head. He loved me and I had never questioned that, but his actions put me in a bad head space. He was doing all that he could to make sure that I could trust him again. It was up to me to accept it and I was trying. I think what I needed was time away from him and everything. Maybe a night out with my girls to clear my head.

I picked up the phone and sent a group text to everyone, and everyone agreed, except Reign. I should have known she would say no.

She was going whether she wanted to or not.

I finished up the paperwork for my last client, and a knock came at the door. I knew it was Reign, so I didn't bother to say come in. The person knocked again and I told them to come in. When I looked up, I saw that it was Jerimiah, who I now knew was the husband of the bitch that Christian slept with.

"Why are you here?"

"I just wanted to talk to you about your husband and my wife."

"I don't need you to tell me anything about my man," I snarled up my nose. "You worry about that whore of a wife of yours, I got Christian."

"So I take it you already know they are sleeping together."

"WERE!" I yelled unintentionally.

"Are you sure of that?" he smirked and I wanted to shoot him in the face.

"Yes, I am. Your wife may be fucking around but it's not with my man!"

He didn't say anything, he just sat there like he was thinking about shit. I got his ass with that statement. I knew for a fact that Christian wasn't fucking around with her because I had tracking on his phone and I knew everywhere he went. I didn't fully trust him yet, so I needed back up evidence.

"Do you know that you being with a criminal could cost you your whole practice and everything that you worked so hard for? Because I can assure you he is going down, and if you are with him, you're going down too."

I tilted my head to the side and took in his appearance for a second before I opened my desk drawer and pulled out my baby .380 that was there for situations just like this.

I pulled it out and took the safety off. I set it on my desk and his eyes got wide as shit. He acted like he wanted to run, but I wasn't having that. If he thought that he was going to try and come in here and threaten me because his wife was a whore, he had another thing coming.

"SIT DOWN!" I yelled when he jumped up and made a beeline to the door.

"Look, I didn't come here for all of that. I just wanted to let you know what your man had been up to. I'll just leave now."

"No, you will leave when or if I allow you to." Now, I was pissed off and he was the cause of it, so he was about to feel my wrath. "Have a seat, Mr. Straggs. Now, was that a threat?"

"Ohhhhhh, you're one of those rider chicks, huh?"

I chambered a bullet and slammed the gun back on the desk to let him know that I was not playing with his bowtie wearing ass. He looked like he was about to piss himself and that made me laugh. I guess he thought I was a weak bitch like his wife.

"Are you threatening me?"

"No, I just wanted to know why you were risking your life for a common thug?"

I hopped up so fast and headed over to where he was sitting. I stood directly in front of him and pointed the gun at his head; he swallowed so hard that I could hear it. I wanted him to know that I was not playing with him.

"Now, here's what's going to happen. You are going to get the hell out of my office and you are never going to come back. You will never speak of me or Christian again. And if I find out you did, it's lights out for you."

I strutted to the door and opened it. I never realized that he shut the door until just then. I looked at him and he had tears in his eyes.

"You are free to go. Have a nice day, Mr. Straggs, and remember what we talked about."

He got up without another word and exited my office. I was so mad that I didn't know what to do. This was all Christian's fault. Had he kept his fucking dick in his pants, then none of this shit would be happening right now. I got muthafuckas coming to my place of business talking about where he was sticking his dick, and I was tired of it. All this shit that was happening right now was because of his bad decisions.

"Carol, reschedule all of my appointments for the rest of the day and I will see you on Monday," I told my receptionist.

I was done for the day; I wasn't in the mood to talk to anyone else.

I left work and spent about six hours in the mall getting in some retail therapy. My phone had been going off since I left the office. It was no one but Christian, and I wasn't ready to talk to him just yet.

The mall was fairly crowded that day. It was Friday and mostly everyone was getting ready to do what I was doing myself—getting prepared to go shake my ass without a care in the world.

I had picked an all-black romper that tapered around my ankle, and ballooned out just a little and hugged my size 14 hips just right. The cleavage part of the romper was cut fairly low. I knew that if Christian saw that shit, he would probably cut it the fuck up.

CJ was spending the night with his nana, so I had no worries with him. Christian said that he and the guys had business to tend to, so I was free to do me tonight. I exited the mall, headed in the direction of the highway with no destination. I knew the one place I wasn't going, and that was home. I had no desire to see Christian right now.

After driving around for a while, I decided to stop to go ahead and head to Jess's house. Ma Ron and Karen were watching all the kids tonight at Ma Karen's house, so no one had kids. I called everyone up and told them that we were meeting at Jess's.

When I pulled in the driveway, I noticed that Shamaad's truck was still there. I just put my head down because I was not in the mood for his got damn mouth. I went to put the car in reverse so that I could back up, but he opened the door and saw me.

He had his phone to his ear and was talking super loud.

"Yeah, bruh, her water head ass is right here. You wanna talk to her?" he asked, looking at me, smiling.

He got on my damn nerves.

"Yeah dog, she gotta lot of shopping bags in the back."

He looked deeper in to the car.

"Got damn nigga, what you do?"

I got out the car and grabbed my bags. I headed to the trunk to get my shoes.

Shamaad followed me and started whistling.

"Nigga, yo' black card is through."

I laughed and walked past him into the house. "They call themselves going out. Oh, you didn't know." I could hear Christian flipping the fuck out. "Telllleeeepphooonnneeee," Shamaad sang.

I hated him sometimes.

I walked up, snatched the phone out of his hand and he snatched it back. "You better take yo' midget ass on somewhere snatching shit before I bop you on yo' head."

"Just give me the damn phone, Maad." He finally handed me the phone.

"Yes, Christian?"

"Oh, you going out tonight and didn't plan on telling nobody?"

"I just want to go out with my girls and have a good time, that's all. What is the harm in that?"

"Did I say it was a muthafuckin problem? Huh? I don't know what the fuck wrong with you today, but I ain't with the shit. Now we been doing good and all of a sudden you want to flip the fucking script. What the fuck I do now?"

"You got muthafuckas coming to my job and shit threatening me because of you?"

"What the fuck do you mean, Ivy? And why the fuck am I just now hearing about this?"

"Jerimiah Straggs. Keri's husband showed up to my office on some you gon' lose all you work for if you keep dealing with him because you're going down. I'm tired of this bitch. You told me that you were going to handle it and for me to leave it alone, but I see the shit ain't handled and I'm still being affected by it."

"Baby, I'm sorry, I swear I am. I'm working on it right now."

"Well, while you're working on it, I'm going out with my friends."

"Yo Ivy, don't do nothing stupid, remember what I told you. It's not a fucking joke!" he screamed.

"Nigga, I ain't you," I said, and then hit the end button.

I handed Shamaad back his phone. I didn't know why he was mugging me and I didn't want to know. "Snitch ass nigga."

"You got damn right, and I will be reporting the entire time you here."

I just rolled my eyes and went in the house to find Jess. I was not about to let either one of them ruin my night. I was on a mission to let my hair down and chill with my girls and that was exactly what I was going to do.

I was over Christian and his bullshit. I was trying to let shit go, but it seemed like every time I did, something else happened. First, there was the bitch getting him arrested and now the bitch's husband was showing up at my job and shit. I loved his ass too much, but all this drama was starting wear me down. He had two choices and two only: handle this situation or let me go.

After about an hour or so of being here, the rest of the girls arrived. They were all hype, except for one. Reign was totally against it and so were the guys, but they would be fine. We were all dressed and looking good. Shamaad's ass thought he was slick. I saw him come in here with that got damn phone.

"Girl, I'm telling you, you start some shit, I'm getting in yo' ass," said Reign's ass. She was so scared that big bad Messiah was going to get in her ass. "You and Christian need to stop this crazy shit."

"Oh stop, Reign, I just want to go out and have a drink with my damn girls."

"Whatever, bitch, I know you," and that was the end of the conversation.

If Christian would have seen what I had on, he would flip

shit. It had only been six weeks since I had my baby but I had lost all my baby weight and I was back down to the weight that I was before I got pregnant. I was so happy that I didn't hold on to that weight. I was about to turn some heads and make some bitches mad tonight.

"You know they gon' have somebody out there with us, right?" Jess asked, shaking her head and looking towards the door.

I looked in the direction that she was looking in and noticed that Shamaad was standing there with a stupid look on his face.

"They should just leave us alone," I rolled my eyes and walked around the counter; big mistake. Shamaad took a picture.

"Shamaad, do not send that picture."

"Bruh, she don't want you to see what she has on." I hated Shamaad sometimes. "Nope, Reign ain't dressed no better, hold on." He tried to take a picture of Reign, but she got out of the kitchen and into the bathroom before he could.

"Messiah said if I can't take a picture of your outfit then you can bring your ass home."

"Don't you have somewhere to be?" Jess asked Shamaad.

"You shut the hell up before I go get my spray tan and orangify yo' ass! Keep it up, you know I will."

"You get on my nerves. I swear I hate you sometimes."

"You can show me how much you hate this sweet meat later."

He grabbed his crotch.

"EEEWWWWWWW," me, Amya, Amila, and Reign all said in unison.

Shamaad flipped us off and walked towards the door.

"Don't do nothing that you wouldn't want us to see," he said, and the way he said it made me believe that they were definitely going to have someone watching us.

With the way that I felt, I was down to put on a show.

Chapter Twenty-Four

CHRISTIAN

onight we were meeting Snake at Onyx to talk
business. We reached out and offered him a deal
that he couldn't refuse. Once we told him who we were and
what we did, he was eager to work with us. A little too eager if
you ask me, but everyone thought I was paranoid. Something
wasn't right about him though, and I didn't like it.

Keith had been quiet. He missed his day to re-up and that
wasn't like him. So that had me a little on edge too. He had
another day to contact us or we were going hunting, and he
would not like that outcome of that.

I had no idea why Messiah suggested Onyx, but the
second I heard the "Ayyyyeeee," I knew exactly why. In walked
all of the women. I looked over at Ivy and she was clearly
drunk. Tonight was going to be a long night.

"I'ma fuck Jess ass up, look at the shit she got on,"

Shamaad fussed and jumped up out of his seat. "She must have changed that shit after I left. Aight, she wanna play? Watch what's gon' happen. I'ma lock her ass in that tanning bed I just bought her ass."

He was always talking shit about her being white but let someone else say something, he would be ready to shoot their ass. They still didn't know that we were there.

They sat on the other side of the club in the VIP section. We were in the cut where no one could see us unless we wanted to be seen.

"What time is this nigga supposed to be here?" I asked, getting impatient.

"I don't know, but ain't that Ivy's ex over there by the entrance?"

"Fuck yeah," I jumped up and Messiah grabbed my arm. I jerked away, ready to go over there and show my ass.

"Wait nigga, just watch his ass. You're moving on emotion."

He was right, because with the way I was feeling right now, I would just go over there in the middle of the club and shoot him in the head. I needed to be level headed with this.

I sat back and just kept my eyes open. I was in a position to see Ivy and everything she did, and I could see if that nigga made a move. I would chill for right now.

A few minutes went by and in walked this black ass nigga with bright ass clothes on. He had on so many jewels that I thought that I was part of a jewelry heist.

"Please don't let that be this nigga," I said to no one in particular.

They all laughed. I guess they knew something I didn't. I was serious as hell. I hated working with show off ass niggas. They were the ones that would get you caught the fuck up. When he headed our way, all I could do was shake my head.

"What's up fellas, I'm Snake," he reached his hand out and everyone shook it, except for me.

I didn't know what the fuck that nigga did with his hands. I just threw him a head nod and moved in behind Messiah and Shamaad to give that nigga somewhere to sit.

"Ya bodyguard or some shit?"

They laughed. I didn't see shit funny, I wanted to shoot him too. I didn't even bother commenting, I just looked over at the girls' section. They had an area full of strippers and they were making it rain. I was just glad that they were happy. I looked around for that fuck boy, and I didn't see him. I didn't like that shit, I wanted to have eyes on him.

I grabbed my phone and called the homie that was outside keeping look out, and told him if he saw that nigga to call me. Everyone knew what he looked like because I made sure of it, so that if he ever came near Ivy, they would know to blast on sight.

We talked business with this clown for a good hour. He kept trying to low ball us until Messiah just got pissed and said fuck it. The deal was off. I told him not to fuck with him anyway, I knew something wasn't right about that nigga. Now we were going to have to off his ass.

What pissed me off even more was on his way out of the door, he stopped in the girls' area and tried to rap with one of them. They all cussed his ass out. The look he gave them gave me a weird feeling. I would make sure I had someone following the girls' home to make sure that they got there safe.

"I'm glad he don't know who the fuck y'all are," Messiah said, speaking on the fact that they were hired by Snake to take out Keith.

"No one does. That would defeat the purpose of what we do, nigga," Raheem said.

"The only way someone would know who the Calvary was if they are about to die; other than that, I'm Shaheed and that's Raheem."

That shit was going to work in our favor because they were hired to take out Keith's bitch ass, and as soon as they get their money, we were killing Snake's bitch ass. But first, I needed to handle Jerimiah's ass for that stunt he pulled with Ivy earlier today.

"Aye, you got that info on that lawyer nigga?"

"Yep, that nigga at his house right now. I tapped into that nigga's phone and I'm tracking his shit. He been there for the last few hours," Raheem said, checking his watch. "You ready to go handle that?"

"Yeah, just let me go tell Ivy bye and to have a good time."

"I'm going too," Messiah laughed.

We walked over to the girls' area and they were still oblivious that we were there. They were too enthralled with what was going on in front of them.

I walked in the area and stood behind Ivy. She didn't move and I got pissed. What if there was another nigga standing behind her? I grabbed her by the shoulder and spun her around; she was laughing, but I wasn't.

"The fuck are you doing letting niggas run up behind you like that?"

"Shut up, Christian, I knew it was you."

"How the fuck you know it was me?"

"Because I watched yo' ass walk over here."

"How?"

"The mirror, dumb ass."

I looked up, and sure enough there was a mirror where you could see everything, even our little section that we were sitting in.

"So you knew I was here the whole time?"

"Duh," they all laughed and I just shook my head.

We taught them to always be aware of their surroundings, especially in our line of business. We had to always be prepared.

I gave her a kiss on the lips, slapped her ass and started towards the exit.

"Where are you going?"

"To handle something, I will be home before you," I yelled over the music. "Be in *our* bed when I get there too. If not, there will be hell to pay."

She smiled, "I'll think about it."

"There is nothing to think about it. If you are not in that bed, you will suffer the consequences and there's a lot pent up, so I suggest you do what the hell I say."

"Goodbye, Christian."

"You heard what the fuck I said, Ivy."

"Oooooohhhhhhhhhhhh," all the girls sang in unison to my threat.

"Y'all can kiss my damn ass!" she yelled at them.

"You just do what I said, and be naked too." She flipped me off and I laughed. "Y'all be careful and be on the lookout."

With that, we left and headed to handle some business. I wanted to hurry up so I could get home before Ivy changed her mind.

Chapter Twenty-Five

IVY

I was done with this fighting with Christian. After he fucked my brains out tonight, we were going to have a long conversation about us. I needed to know if we were going to be together or not. I was tired of the back and forth with us. Ever since he found out the abortion, things have been downhill for us since then. I wanted to be with him, but we needed to have an understanding first.

He needed to understand that I was not about to put up with him cheating when he decided he wanted to get all mad and shit. If he was mad, then he needed to go in another room or go for a run or something, but running up into random pussy was not going to work for me. I would forgive him this time because I loved him that much, but I be damned if I sit around for that shit again, and I needed him to understand that.

"Alright party animal, you ready to go?" Reign asked.

"Yeah, I'm ready to go home and see my man. It's been forever since I felt that dick in the back of my throat."

"Nasty bitch," Reign frowned and we all laughed.

"Oh hell, y'all were thinking that shit. I just said it."

"I'm glad y'all are working on y'all shit because I was tired of this shit."

"You and me both."

We walked outside and the air hit me like a ton of bricks. It was a little chilly out and I was sweaty from all the dancing and money throwing. I took in my surroundings because something didn't feel right. It was like someone was watching me or something.

"It feels like someone is watching us, y'all."

The girls looked around and we all grabbed our purses. Nothing looked out of the ordinary, but you never knew. That was the one thing that I hated about them being in the game, I hated having to watch my back every day. I couldn't wait until the day they were out of the game for good.

We piled in Reign's SUV and we were headed to Jess's house where the cars were. We had the music on and we were still in party mode. I was happy that I was going to make love to the man I loved tonight for the first time in what seemed like forever.

"That van has been following us since we left the club," Amya said, grabbing her phone. "We're being followed by a white van with tinted windows. What do you want us to do?"

Right after she asked, the van rear ended us. Nobody

screamed because we weren't built that way. But we all reached for our guns and then they hit us again. Reign was being a champ, holding that SUV in the road with one hand while she was preparing to shoot out the window with the other.

"They are rear ending us but Reign is holding this shit like a champ," Amya boasted. "Okay, we will. I love you too," she said as she unbuckled her seat belt and put her phone in her bra while it was still on. "I need all of you to call your men and put you phones in your bras. Get ready to shoot. The guys are finishing up something and then they are on the way."

We all nodded and did what she said. I called Christian, and the minute the call was answered, he started barking out orders. I did everything he told me to do and put the phone in my bra under my titties. I grabbed my baby out of my pocketbook and got ready to do what I needed to do to get home to my family.

"Um, y'all," Jess said.

We already knew what it was, she was the only one who didn't carry a damn gun. She was so hardheaded. We had told her time and time again, you never know what could happen out here. Now what if she was by herself and had her kid?

"Under the seat, Jess, damn!" Reign said and we all laughed, even though there wasn't a damn thing funny about this shit right now.

We were rear ended again and we all hung out the windows and started firing at the van.

"Shoot out the tires!" Amila screamed.

She was steady busting at the windshield. She hit somebody because the van swerved and went off the embankment.

"Fuck yeah!" Reign yelled.

That crazy heffa had been around Messiah too long because she was the only one who got excited about doing shit like that.

"Oh shit!" she screamed as a big ass Suburban came and side swiped us and we hit the guard rail on side of the road.

She slammed on the brakes and we all jumped out.

Click, click, was all that we heard and we all stood still. There was a big ass nigga standing in front of the SUV. The front door of the Suburban swung open and that flamboyant nigga that tried to holla at us, stepped out, clapping his hands.

"Bravo! Take a damn bow! That was some impressive shooting for a bunch of bitches," he laughed, and so did the big nigga that was standing with the AK-47.

"W ap ale nan vle ou pa janm te di ke (You're going to wish you never said that)," Amila said, smiling. "Mwen pa ka tann nan koupe Dick ou koupe ak manje l 'ba ou. (I can't wait to cut your dick off and feed it to you.)"

We all laughed.

"She just said she wanted to suck my dick in another language, you hear that shit, Killa? That was some sexy shit, say it again."

"W ap kòm bèbè jan ou gade (You're as dumb as you look)," Amya added. "Li k ap pase yo dwe plezi touye ou, epi ou twò killa (It's going to be fun killing you, and you too, Killa)."

Again, we laughed. Amila and Amya had started teaching us Haitian Creole after we first met them about a year and half ago so that we would understand them when they were speaking it. We picked up on understanding it great, but speaking it was a whole other ball game. In situations like this, it came in handy.

"Alright, enough of that bullshit. Hell, y'all even got the white bitch speaking that shit."

"Tengo tu perra blanca (I got your white bitch)," Jess said getting pissed.

"Next person that speaks that fufu frafra shit is getting shot."

"That was Spanish, asshole."

"Well how about I light your white ass up and call it a fucking fiesta?"

"Chill, Jess," I told her.

My girl looked like she wanted to go over there and fuck his shit all the way up. In due time, she would get to do what she needed to do.

"Are we just going to stand out here all night or what?"

"Well, you bitches killed my transport van, so I have to wait for someone to come pick you bitches up."

"Sir, is all of that necessary?"

Reign was too calm for my liking. That usually meant that some shit was about to go down. She looked to her left and then back real quick. I think I was the only one that caught it, but she smiled and started talking shit. "How would you like it if I talked about your mother the way you are talking about us?"

"I wouldn't think anything of it, I would just kill you. And if you don't shut the fuck up, I'm going to kill you anyway."

Reign turned around to face us. She rolled her eyes around in a circle and we all smiled. She turned back around and faced them.

"Èske ou pare yo mouri? (Are you ready to die?)" I asked in my best Haitian Creole accent.

"Pafè (Perfect)," Amya and Amila complimented in unison, causing us to giggle.

"Didn't I say the next one of you to start talking that shit was gonna get fucking shot? I guess y'all don't take me serious. Killa, shoot the bitch with the big ass."

"Which one, they all got big asses?"

"Shit, pick one," they laughed and Killa raised his gun, but before he could get it aimed, we all heard *POW* and he hit the ground loud.

The colorful guy attempted to reach for his gun and was stopped by a blow to his face.

"Don't you ever call my white girl no white bitch again, you got that?" Shamaad hit his ass again.

"Aight, chill, let's get him to the House of Pain," Messiah said with that fucked up grin on his face.

"Hold up," Christian said. "Who the fuck put you up to this 'cause you don't know enough about us to want to do this shit on your own. Was it Keith's bitch ass?"

"Fuck you!"

"Baby, he messed up my truck," Reign whined.

"Really, bitch?" I looked at her like she was crazy.

"I'm not talking to you," she crossed her arms and pouted.

"Baby, I will get you another truck tomorrow. Can we please get out the middle of the road? It's four o'clock in the morning and granted the fact that this is a country road, somebody could still ride by."

"Fine!"

This spoiled bitch was about to get slapped.

Messiah shook his head and walked away. They dragged the colorful guy down the road a little bit and into the woods. I had no idea where they came from, but I wasn't questioning it.

We piled back in Reign's car and headed to the House of Pain.

Chapter Twenty-Six

KEITH

I had been hiding from Christian and Messiah for a while now. I never met them for the re-up and I didn't plan too. I reached out to my other connect, Snake, and brought him in on my little plan to kill them and take over. I knew that it was going to be difficult, but I had a way to get to them, and it would crush their entire soul.

My dumb ass daughter was dead set on ruining this for me with that dumb ass stunt she pulled. I was over her and her shenanigans. She was currently staying at the house with me and her mother, so that I could keep an eye on her and keep her away from Christian.

As of lately, she had been talking about some nigga named Ty, so hopefully he would take her mind off of Christian long enough for me to do what I needed to do.

Snake was due to meet with them tonight. He was

supposed to get them to agree to work with him so that we could get that much closer to the women. I was waiting on him to call now so that we could get to work. With them, you had to move fast and careful, because one fuck up and it would cause you your life, and I wasn't trying to die before I got rich.

My phone rang and it was Snake.

"We're good?"

"Nah, change of plans."

"What do you mean change of plans? Shit don't work like that with them, you can't go changing the plan. You have to stick with what we planned."

"I'm running this show and I said that fucking plans have changed."

He hung up the phone and I attempted to call back several times, but I got nothing. I threw my head on my desk and just left it there until I heard my door open.

"I see we are trying to kill the same person, Daddy."

"Get out, Keri. You don't know what you're talking about."

"I just heard your whole conversation."

"Get the fuck out, Keri!"

She just stood there for a minute and I was about to curse her ass out until my phone rang and I hurried and picked it up.

"Snake?"

"We are about to get the girls, meet me at the spot."

He hung up the phone again.

I hated that cocky bastard. I should have never trusted someone with the name Snake. I should have just kept doing what I was doing with Christian and Messiah, instead of being greedy. Too late; now I had to do what I had to do.

I jumped up out of my seat and slapped the piss out of her. I was tired of her and her shit. I was going to end up killing her myself.

"Stay the fuck away from this, or I will kill you."

I pushed her out of my office and locked my door. I ran down the stairs and out the door, speeding all the way to the little warehouse I had in Salisbury, and waited for them to come.

I called a few people from my crew just in case there was going to be a problem. I knew how they operated and it was always best to be prepared. Plus, I didn't trust Snake all the way. I wanted my guys there in case he decided to do something.

I waited for a couple of hours and no one ever showed up. I called Snake a thousand times. I didn't know what the fuck happened, but shit wasn't looking good.

I got my keys and walked outside. I felt safe because I knew that my guys were out there watching and no one could get to me here.

I got in the car and started it up.

"Going somewhere?" I almost pissed myself when I heard the voice.

How the hell did they know where I was and where the fuck was Snake?

"Drive, and if you try any dumb shit, I will blow your brains out. Do you understand?"

"Look Christian, I have your money I just needed a few extra days to get it together. But we can go to my house right now."

"Fuck you, Keith, just follow that truck right there."

"What truck?" I asked, but right after I did, a truck came tearing from the back of my warehouse.

They blew the horn and took off in the direction of the highway.

"There are three cars with us, so if you try something, you will be dead before you can think straight. So, just drive until I tell you to stop."

"Please don't kill me, I'm sorry for what I've done. I will do whatever you need me to do. Just please, don't kill me."

"Drive, muthafucka!"

We drove around for about 45 minutes before he told me to turn down this long dark ass road. I didn't want to do it, but I didn't want to risk not doing it either. They wouldn't kill me, they needed me. So, if I did what they wanted me to do, I would make it out of this. I was done trying to be greedy.

"Pull into that garage and park."

I did what he told me to do. Someone opened my door; I looked up and it was Messiah. He had a smile on his face. During the entire time that I had been working with them, I had never seen that man smile. But today, he was cheesing like he had won the got damn lottery.

"Come on, my friend," Messiah said. He patted me on the

back and led me into this room. It was all white and the only thing that was in the room was a big ass table with two chairs. "Have a seat and make yourself comfortable."

"What's going on, fellas?"

"You will see soon enough. Can we get you anything? A beer? A cigar? Anything?"

"Yeah, a shot of your strongest Cognac!"

"You got it, my friend."

I didn't know what was up with the 'my friend' thing, but I didn't like it. I knew for a fact that muthafucka didn't like me. I was about to find a way out of here. I had to, if I wanted to live. They walked away and left the door wide open. Something was telling me that this was a trick, but I had to try.

I jumped up and ran out of the room, only to get a nice surprise.

"Fuck my life!"

Chapter Twenty-Seven

CHRISTIAN

The look on Keith's face when he walked in the room and seen all of us standing there with Snake tied to the chair was funny as hell. Snake's face was bloodied the fuck up from Shamaad whooping his ass for calling Jess a white bitch. Keith thought we were dumb enough to leave the door open so that he could escape. He didn't know us as well as he thought he did.

"Look fellas, I can explain."

Explaining would do him no good for what we were about to do to him.

"Too late for that, my friend," Messiah said, swinging Louise around in a circle.

I hated that got damn bat. I knew from the first time that he watched the episode of *The Walking Dead* and they showed that damn bat, he was going to have one. Shit was nasty and way too messy for my taste, but that muthafucka loved it and preferred it.

Raheem walked over and escorted Keith to the seat next to Snake. He acted like he wanted to protest, but one jab to the gut made him change his mind. He sat down and mugged Snake. I don't know why he thought going against us was a smart thing to do. He should've checked his facts before he did that.

We heard the door to the building open and close. We all grabbed our guns, ready for whatever was about to come into that door.

Right as we were about to let loose, Reign come bopping around the corner.

"What did we miss?" she said, making her way over to Messiah.

"The short bus," Shamaad said and ducked because he knew something was coming his way as soon as the words left his mouth.

Sure enough, the wristlet that she had on struck him in the head.

"You a fucking bully, Reign," Shamaad pointed at her and shook his head.

She flipped him off.

"You didn't miss anything, baby."

Messiah grabbed her, so she wouldn't go after Shamaad.

"What the hell took you so long to get here?"

"I dropped them by Jess's house to get their cars."

Messiah nodded his head and all I was thinking was that

that would be one less stop we had to make on our way home. I was ready to get into some pussy.

Amila and Amya walked right into the building and past everyone. They were headed straight to the saw room. They looked pissed and I was not about to ask what was wrong. They were not about to flip on me; they were crazy.

Amila came out of the room with a machete and walked right over to where Snake was sitting.

"Do you guys mind?" Amya asked.

"Damn, can we ask him a question first before you try and chop his ass up?" Shamaad mugged her.

She dropped the machete down by her side and gave Shamaad the death stare.

"Fucking devil."

"Poukisa Dont ou fèmen anvan ou piss m 'la. (why don't you shut up before you piss me off)."

"No, fuck that! Speak English, got damn it, I don't understand that Haitian shit! That shit ain't fair! You can't be sitting here talking shit about me and I don't know what the fuck you talking about."

Shamaad was serious as hell.

"Ou se tankou moun sòt (you are such an idiot)."

"Fuck you too, you blue eyed fucker."

I swear they couldn't get along for nothing. They argued like they were brother and sister, no lie. It was crazy how close they all were. By the way they talked to each other, you would never think that, but they were.

""Jis inyore l ', li se espesyal (Just ignore him, he's special),"
Jess said in the same language they were speaking.

Shamaad looked at her like she was crazy. I guess he didn't
know that they had been learning that shit from Amila and
Amya for a while now.

I knew because I had walked in on Ivy speaking that shit
on the phone.

"No hell," he pointed at Jess. "Yo' ass is white, try again."

Why did he have to be so stupid?

"Aight, time to get to work."

I had to stop them or they would go back and forth all
night and I was ready to get home and into Ivy.

I walked over and kissed her on the jaw and she was still
receptive, so I was really ready to get this over with.

"We got dibs on him," Amya pointed to Snake.

"Fuck you, bitch." Messiah raised Louise and was about to
come down on his head, but Amila stopped him.

"No, I got this."

She walked over to him and attempted to get his pants
down. He kicked her, and she raised up and threw like four
good jabs to his face. Then her sister walked over and
helped her.

Once they had his pants successfully down, they asked for
help to stand him up. Their crazy ass husbands went over to
assist because I wasn't. I had a feeling this was about to be
some nasty ass shit. So, I stood back and let them do their
thing.

"I told you that I was going to cut your dick off and feed it to you for calling me a bitch," Amila said, and Snake called her another bitch. "I pride myself on being a woman of my word."

With that, she picked up the machete that she had laid on the table while helping her sister, and with one whack, she cut that man's dick off. I was hurt for that nigga.

She proceeded to shove that man's chopped dick down his throat.

He screamed out as much as he could, but with a dick in his mouth, he couldn't say much.

"You should really learn how to talk to a lady," Amya said and took the machete and sliced his head clean off of his shoulders.

I stood there and looked, because the whole time all of this was going on, not one of them flinched.

I was over here squirming and everything; that was some tough shit to watch as a man. I knew they did jobs together and shit, but damn, I didn't know shit got that deep.

"Are y'all fucking done? Got damn!" Shamaad yelled out, still bent over from the shock of watching her castrate that man.

They just looked at him and smiled. They stepped back and walked off to the back somewhere with Raheem and Shaheed in tow. You had to be a messed up soul to be able to do something like that. I didn't even want to think about what they went through when they were younger to make them the way they were now. Maybe one day I would learn their story, but right now, I'd rather leave it a mystery.

Keith sat there with tears in his eyes, knowing that he was next. He already knew what the consequences were for crossing us, so I don't even know why he tried. All because he went behind our back and tried to short our money.

"So, why would you try and have our girls kidnapped?" I asked him. "And tell the truth because we already know everything."

"It was all Snake's idea. He said that he wanted to take over your territory and that I could just work for him. I didn't want to."

"I think you are lying to me, my friend."

Messiah walked towards him with that got damn bat and I moved back. He laughed like shit was funny, but he knew what the fuck he was doing with that bat.

"Where the fuck you going, Chris?"

"I don't see shit funny, nigga. You know I don't like that shit."

"Pussy," Messiah laughed. "Like I was saying my friend, it sounds like you lied to me. You know I hate liars."

Messiah came up with the bat and connected with his shoulder and he screamed. All you could see was meat hanging from that bat. This nigga held it up and looked at it as if that shit was normal. He shook his head and came down on him again and again, until there was nothing left of him but bones and mush. That was some nasty shit. I literally had to walk away. If it was left up to me, I would have just shot him in the head and called it a day, but that would be too easy for Messiah's twisted ass.

"We'll catch y'all twisted asses later."

I chucked the deuces, grabbed Ivy's hand, and we left out of the building. I was just ready to get home and make love to my woman. I was crazy, but I was nowhere near as crazy as what the hell I had just watched.

"Come the hell on Shamaad so I can get you home," Jess laughed because Shamaad was still reliving the castrating part. "See y'all."

We all walked out and got in my car. I would have to come get her car tomorrow. Shamaad's ass was in a trance, so he didn't even say goodbye. He just stared straight ahead. I couldn't do anything but laugh.

The ride home was filled with silence and I wanted to spark up a conversation, but I didn't want to argue myself out of a session with my girl, so I stayed quiet.

Ivy kept moving around in her seat like she had something on her mind.

"Talk to me, baby," I threw out there.

"I have to know that this shit won't happen again. I need for you to make me believe that it's just me and you 'til the end."

"These last few months or so have been hell for me, not being able to touch you, talk to you, confide in you, nothing. I truly felt like I lost my best friend and I was lost as hell. You are my everything, Ivy. I need you like I need water in my body to live. Without you, there is no me, and that's real talk."

I wanted her to feel every word.

"I would never do anything to jeopardize my family again,

you have to believe me. I need you, Ivy. I would take my own life before I hurt you again."

She said nothing. She just sat there with tears running down her face. I didn't know what was going through her head, but I needed to know that she knew I was for real. I didn't want to push her though.

I gave her a minute; the car was filled with an uncomfortable silence the rest of the way to the house. When we got the house, I pulled my truck into the driveway and put it in park.

Ivy opened her door to get out, but I grabbed her arm. She turned and looked at me and I couldn't read her expression.

"I meant everything I said."

Again, she said nothing. All she did was close the door back and turned facing me in the truck.

"I love you with everything in me and you know that. Please don't ever take that for granted again. If you ever hurt me again, you won't get a chance to take your own life because I'm going to take it for you."

I just nodded my head because I knew that she was speaking straight from the heart on that one.

"Now I'm not gon' say I'ma be perfect because I am sure that I will fuck up, but it will never be with another woman again. Can you deal with that?"

She looked at me like she was thinking, and then she smiled and nodded her head. That was all I needed. I felt like I was on top of the world with that one notion. I leaned over, grabbed the back of her head and kissed her with every ounce of passion that I had to give.

The second she moaned into my mouth, I lost it. I started ripping at her clothes and mine. Once we were both naked, I slid the seat to my truck all the way back and motioned for her to join me.

"Let's just go in the house."

"Get your ass over here, Ivy."

She bit her lip and did what the hell I said. She mounted my lap and put my head at her opening, and eased down real slow. It had been a minute, so I knew that she needed to get use to my size again.

I leaned forward and found her nipple while she moved around a little, trying to get all of me to fit.

I ran my tongue around her areola, causing her nipple to get hard as fuck.

"Ummmmmmmmmm," she moaned and I lifted up out of my seat a little to help her out. Maybe she was right, fucking in the car for the first time in months may have not been the brightest of ideas. "Sssssssss, God, I missed you."

"Well show me then, baby," I whispered in her ear.

She threw her head back and started bouncing on my shit.

I pushed her back some so that I could get my hands on her clit. I needed to feel it—it had been far too long. Once I put pressure on her clit, she really started moving. I had to concentrate on something else because I swear I was going to cum at any minute; that shit was feeling too good.

"Fuck, baby," I moaned out.

Ivy had always been a "rider," but tonight I think she had something to prove. She started grinding on my shit and making circles with her hips. I just knew I was about to let go. Right when I was at my peak, she stopped.

"What the fuck you stop for?"

"Did you hear that?"

"I didn't hear shit. The only thing I'm trying to hear is the sound of how wet yo' pussy is coming down on my dick."

I opened the door and stepped out of the truck while still inside her. She wrapped her arms around my neck like I was going to drop her. I placed her back against my truck and put her legs in the crooks of my arms. I started moving in and out of her real slow. I leaned down to kiss her and she gave me the kiss of a lifetime, something that I had been missing these last few months.

"Ohhhhh baby, that feels so good."

"Ummm hummmm, you are so fucking wet."

"Just for you baby, just for you! Uhhhhhhhnhhhhhh."

Hearing that sparked something in me. I leaned back a little so I could watch my dick disappear in her awaiting tunnel.

"Just look at this shit, all fucking mine." I sped up just enough to make her eyes roll into the back of her head. "How could I ever be so dumb? Just listen to how wet you are."

"Shitttttttttt, daddy, I'm about to cum."

"Give it to daddy, I need to feel you cum all over my dick."

"Sssss, yeah, yeah, yeah, yeah," she screamed, and at that moment, I thank God that we didn't have close neighbors because they would have been front and center watching the show.

I lifted her some to get a better grip, then I lifted her and slammed her down on my dick. I was almost at my climax. Ivy was screaming out of control at that point and I could have sworn I heard a door shut, but I was not trying to find out until after I busted this nut.

"Fuck, baby, I'm 'bout to nut," I sped up. And I know I was making some ugly ass faces, I would just have to hear about it later 'cause I couldn't control that shit if I tried.

"Oooohhhh shit, me too, baby, me too."

Her pussy muscles clamped around my dick and I lost it. I let off every kid that was left in my sac. I hoped she was ready for another kid because her ass got pregnant with that one. I was trying to recover when I saw a figure move to my left. I spun around, shielded Ivy's body and came face to face with the barrel of a .22.

"What the fuck are you doing here. Ty?" Ivy yelled, trying to come out from around me.

She was pissed the fuck off, but this crazy ass nigga had a gun and I was not about to risk him shooting her. I would take a bullet for her any day.

"Did you hear me, nigga?"

"Because I tried to talk to you, Ivy, and you wouldn't listen. I thought that after I showed you those pictures, you would leave him and come be with me, but you didn't, you stayed."

Tears were actually running down his face.

In any other instance, I would have laughed in his face, but I held it together.

"You left me because I cheated, but he cheated and you stayed?"

"You had a whole fucking wife and family, so what do you mean? Wait, why am I even trying to explain anything to you? Just get the fuck away from my house before you make me mad."

"Calm down, Ivy. Once he is out of the way, you will see that you are happier with me."

"Let me get my clothes, Christian," she gritted. I knew that she was mad, hell, I was too. How the fuck did he know where I live and how long had he been watching? "I hope you liked the show, you fucking bastard."

"Do you know how painful it is to see the woman I love fuck someone else?"

This muthafucka was crazy and when I had a clear shot, I was snatching his gun out of his hand and killing him with it.

I felt Ivy moving behind me, but I didn't know what the hell she was doing. This muthafucka looked unstable as fuck and I didn't want him to fucking shoot, so I needed her ass to be still.

"What the fuck are you doing, Ivy? Stay still before I shoot!" he yelled and she stopped moving, but I could hear her breathing heavy.

That was one woman who hated to be told what to do, unless it was in the bedroom.

"Ty, I don't know who the fuck you think you talking to,

but you know I don't play that shit. You better tone that shit down before you piss me the fuck off."

His attention was on Ivy and that was the perfect time.

"I'm the one with the gun here, so everybody just shut the fuck up!"

"Are you sure about that?" I asked him and rushed his ass.

I grabbed that hand that he was holding the gun with and I heard it go off. I took my free hand and hit his ass in the nose. He naturally let go of the gun to grab his nose. Pussy muthafucka.

"Please, just kill me, I can't live without Ivy," this punk muthafucka cried.

"With pleasure." I gave him one to the dome.

I should have killed his ass a long time ago.

I needed to call the cleanup crew to come clean up the mess we made. We needed to get the body out from in front of our yard just in case someone rode by, not that anyone would be seeing, considering the time of morning it was and where we lived, but we needed to cover our asses.

We dragged the body in the garage and waited for the crew.

I had been staying with my dad since the day Jerimiah caught me with Ty in our house. I had yet to come back home because I was afraid of what he might do. I had been staying at a hotel since the night my dad slapped me. I was on a mission to take him down, along with Christian and Jerimiah.

Ty acted like he didn't want anything to do with me after that day. He stopped taking my calls, and when I popped up at his apartment the other day, it looked empty. I guess all of that with Jerimiah walking in on us was too much.

I sat and stared at my phone as Jerimiah was calling for the millionth time. I was scared to talk to him. I knew that when he got his hands on me, this time was going to be serious. Only problem was that I needed some clothes, and I was running out of money. I thought about answering to make sure that he was at work, but before I could decide, the phone stopped and then there was a knock at the door.

I jumped because I was worried that it could be him, but how would he know where I was? Then I remembered that I had texted Ty and told him where I was, so I jumped up and checked the mirror to make sure that I was presentable.

I opened the door and immediately tried to slam it shut.

"I take it my wife doesn't want to see me?" Jerimiah asked.

"Look, I'm sorry; I don't know what came over me, but I'm sorry, and it will never happen again."

"But you looked like you were having so much fun," he smirked.

I backed away from him because I didn't like the way he was looking at me. He looked like he was high, or out of his mind or something.

"What's wrong with you? Why are you here?"

"Your fucking father, where is he?"

"I have no idea, why?"

"Because the motherfucker set me up. With all the crooked shit he was doing, he turned that shit around on me. Him and that crooked ass cop—he planted shit in the house, in my office, everywhere. The police are looking for me right now as we speak."

"I think you should go and turn yourself in, don't make things harder on yourself."

"I needed to see my beloved wife first and tell her how much I loved her whoring ass. I mean with everything my lawyer said they found, I doubt I see the light of day again."

"Just leave, Jerimiah, don't make things worse."

"If I'm going to go to jail and lose everything, it's going to be for a reason."

He sounded slightly off.

He took off the jacket that he had on and came out of his shoes. He dropped his pants and his dick was hard as a brick. He looked down at it and back up at me, then broke out into a fit of laughter.

I bolted to the door, only to be met with the back of his hand.

"You are going to fuck me like you fucked that nigga in my house."

Jerimiah was starting to scare me because he had never talked like that before. I was so used to the proper and well-spoken, now he sounded like the men that he defended. "Plus, all of this is your fault."

"How is this my fault, Jerimiah? I never did anything to you, except be a good wife."

"Had you stayed away from that drug dealer, I would have never gone after him, and we would not be in this situation right now."

"You cheated on me every chance you got, and you thought that I was supposed to just sit at home and be your fool?"

"Yes!"

Whap, whap!

He slapped the shit out of me twice. "That's what the fuck you were supposed to do."

"Please stop, just leave," I cried, hoping that I would get some kind of sympathy from him, but he wasn't having it.

"I want to sample this," he grabbed me under my nighty that I had on, "one last time. Now get over here and if I have to say it again, I'm going to hurt you." He pulled out a gun from the jacket pocket of the jacket he had on. "Try anything I don't like and I will kill you."

I didn't say anything. At that point, the only thing that I could do was what he asked me. He told me to drop to my knees, as he stood in front of me and rubbed his dick on my lips. Then, he slapped me across my lips with it.

"Suck it, and if you bite me I will shoot you." He took the gun and moved my hair out of my face with it. "And play with your pussy too; make it nice and wet because I just snorted a hell of a lot of coke and we got a long night ahead of us."

I knew something was different about him, I could just tell. He wasn't the same Jerimiah that I was used to. I wondered if he had just started this shit or whether it was something that he had been doing.

"How long have you been on drugs?"

"Not that it's any of your business, but Bianca introduced me to it and I figured that I would need it for what I have to do today."

"What do you have to do?" I was scared as hell.

"If you don't suck my dick and play with your pussy, I'm gon' be blowing your brains out." He laughed so loud that I was surprised no one called security. I was low key wishing that they would. "Now get to sucking."

I gathered as much saliva that I could in my mouth and took his dick to the back of my throat. I envisioned that he was Ty. I couldn't think of Christian right now because I wanted him dead.

I closed my eyes and thought about the way that curved dick touched my soul.

"Shit, had you sucked my dick like this before, I would have never had to cheat on you."

Jerimiah was losing it. I hoped like hell I made it out of this. Maybe if I fucked him real good, he would pass out and then I could sneak out and get help. Yeah, that's what I would do. I put my neck all in it and really went to work on his dick. You would have thought I was applying for a role as a porn star.

"Damn, girl," he laughed.

I worked on his rod for a good half an hour, pulling out all kinds of tricks, and nothing. He was enjoying it, but that was it. He was nowhere near close to letting go and I think he was starting to notice what I was doing because he grabbed me by my hair and threw me on the bed.

"Unnuhhhhunnnn," he said, waving his finger back and forth. "I know what you are trying to do and it won't work. Now spread 'em." He flung my legs wide open and ran his fingers down my slit. "You know what? You get on top; I want to feel whatever the fuck that nigga was feeling in order to sit there and disrespect me in my house like that."

"Jerim—" I started, but was quieted by a slap to the face.

Tears began to roll down my face because my chance of getting out of here alive was starting to look slim.

"Do what the fuck I said do."

He laid back and I got on top of him. I slid down on him and began to rock slowly. He cocked his hand back and slapped me again. I grabbed my face and looked at him. I placed my hands flat on his chest and began to bounce up and down real fast. I was winding my ass in a circle and everything. He grabbed my waist and was thrusting upward to meet my moves.

"You were doing all that hollering when that nigga was in you, why I don't hear shit?"

"Oh yesssssss, oh God, yesssss," I moaned. The moan was fake, but my body was actually responding to him, even though I didn't want it to. "Fuck, I'm 'bout to cum."

"Hell yeah, I feel that shit, let it go. Hell, it will be the last nut for the both of us."

When he said that, I panicked and reached back and grabbed the gun that he had on the table. I stopped and pointed it at him.

He looked at me and laughed.

"You wouldn't shoot me."

I pulled the trigger.

Click!

I looked down at the gun and pulled it again. *Click*, and again, *click, click, click, click*. He snatched the gun out of my hand and hit me across the head with it.

I fell over on to the bed.

He jumped up, walked over to the jacket and pulled out a handful of bullets. I just began to sob at that point. I watched him load the gun and just knew it was my time.

"You just don't listen, do you?"

He spread my legs again and roughly inserted himself into my sex.

"Please Jerimiah, don't do this!" I cried.

"Well, act like you like it."

I spread my legs more to give him better access. He started working himself in and out of me. For kicks, I started moaning.

"I can't believe that you actually tried to kill me," he began to laugh again.

He wrapped his hands around my throat and lightly squeezed. He sped up his motions and was starting to get another reaction out of my body without my consent. I wanted so badly to just lay there, but my pussy was deceiving me.

"Ohhhhhh, you like that, don't you? You about to cum again," he released one of his hands from around my neck and rubbed my clit, bringing me closer to my climax. "I'm about to give you the biggest orgasm you have ever had. You ready?" He placed more pressure on my clit. "Answer me!" he yelled.

I nodded my head as I started getting a tingling feeling in the bottom of my toes.

He placed his hands back on my neck and started pounding away. His grip was a little more than what I was comfortable with. The more he pounded, the tighter he squeezed. I started scratching at his arms, and then all of a sudden, my legs started to shake and my eyes rolled in the back of my head. I was experiencing something that I had never felt before. He was right; this was the best orgasm I ever had.

I guess he was cumming too because he started that grunting thing that he did when he was about to cum. After we both came, I was ready for him to release my neck, but he had other plans.

"I told you that would be the best you have ever had; too bad it will be your last." He began to squeeze my neck and I was squirming and scratching, but the way we were positioned, I couldn't move much. Plus, he was still inside of me. "No worries dear, I will see you in hell because I refuse to go to jail."

He squeezed so tight, I couldn't breath and after a while, I gave up. I closed my eyes and I asked the Lord to forgive me, as I drifted off into an eternal sleep.

Chapter Twenty-Nine

IVY

Tonight, was the night of the grand opening of Club Dynasty, and I couldn't be more excited for them. They deserved this and so much more. So much had happened in the last few months, and honestly, I didn't know how we got through any of it, but we did, and were stronger than ever.

The night after we got rid of Ty, we saw on the news that Keri's husband strangled her hoe ass and then turned the gun on himself. They later said that he was facing charges of being a kingpin. That Uncle Tom ass nigga a kingpin? Yeah, somebody set his ass up good.

I was mad as hell because I wanted to be the one to put the bitch out of her misery, but someone beat me to it. She got everything that she deserved and so had Ty.

I just wanted to live happily ever after with my man and

my kids. Yes, I said kids because I was currently pregnant right now. I knew that night in the yard he was going to get my pregnant. I was a little worried because CJ was just four months and we were having another baby, but I guessed we would work it out. It seemed as if and Reign and I were running a race because she found out she was pregnant about three months ago, and Messiah was happy as hell.

Jess was the only one still holding on to not having any more kids yet, but that was because she got hit with two in the beginning.

Christian was out running around, trying to get stuff ready for the party tonight, but I couldn't wait to tell him. I told him that he needed to get home ASAP and that it was important. After I told him, I hung up the phone and wouldn't answer when he called. I knew that was wrong, but that was a guaranteed way to get him home. I knew that his ass was going to be pissed, but that was nothing a nice shot of pussy wouldn't cure.

"Ivy," he huffed as he ran into the house. "Ivy, baby, answer me."

"I'm upstairs," I said in the sweetest voice I could muster up.

I knew he was going to flip shit, so I made sure that I was naked when he got there. Once he got up the stairs, I was standing in the middle of the room with a gift bag and all my naked glory.

"Hey, baby."

He looked at me like he wanted to tear my head off. I

wanted to laugh, but I knew that at this point it would only make things worse, so I held it in and got ready for this tongue lashing, and not in a good way.

"Why the fuck would you do that, Ivy? You already knew that I would think something was wrong. Why would you scare me like that? I thought someone had hurt you." He sounded like he was about to cry, and I really started to feel like shit. "You don't do shit like that, IVY, WHAT THE FUCK!"

He screamed that last part so loud that I jumped.

"I know, but there was something that I needed to tell you and it's important, and I know that you were busy and would only come if it was an emergency."

"I would stop the world for you. You don't have to pretend like it's an emergency to get my attention. Nothing is more important than my family—not this club and damn sure not these streets."

I nodded my head and then handed him the bag. He slid off his shoes and sat on the bed. He opened the bag and tore out all of the paper, and started pulling stuff out. First it was the Sugar Babies, then a Sugar Daddy, a Baby Ruth, Cry Babies, and then the Sour Patch Kids.

He looked at me with one eyebrow up like he wanted to curse me out. I guess he didn't get the hint so I nodded to the bag; he still had one more thing to pull out.

He reached down in the bag and pulled out the sonogram. There were no words to describe the look on his face as he held that sonogram up in the air. My man was so happy he didn't know what to do.

"My baby is giving me another baby?"

I nodded.

He ran his hand across my stomach and then looked up at me. He stood up and wrapped his arms around my waist. He leaned down and kissed me with everything he had and I reciprocated. I grabbed the back of his head to deepen the kiss, but he stopped me. I gave him a look that said he better stop playing.

"Chill out, girl, damn," he smiled.

God, that smile was everything to me.

"I was about to say, what the hell."

He laughed and disappeared into the closet. He came back out with a little black box in his hand and I just covered my mouth with my hands and let the water works begin.

"I should have done this almost a year ago." He got down on one knee in front of me. "I don't know where I would be without you and I never want to find out. Those few months without your love had a nigga feeling lost as hell and I never want to do that again. I don't want to go another day without you being my wife. Will you marry me?"

I couldn't even respond; I just shook my head. He placed the ring on my finger and I cried bloody murder. He kept laughing and trying to shush me, but I was sobbing out of control. He pushed me on my shoulder, which caused me to sit down on the bed. He pushed my shoulder again for me to lay back; the entire time I was crying out of control.

I felt his warm, thick tongue slide across my clit, and I had to let out a moan in between my sobbing. His tongue circled my clit over and over and I almost lost it. Then he flicked his tongue real fast and my moans completely took over the room. The feeling that I was feeling at that moment was unreal.

I grabbed the back of his head because that teasing was not going to work for me. He latched on my clit and started eating like he hadn't in days. I made sure to feed him all he wanted. I was throwing it all in his face and he was lapping every bit of it up. I could definitely do this forever.

After about two straight hours of lovemaking in every imaginable position and even in the shower, we were now getting dressed to go open the doors of our club. Once we got outside, the stretch Hummer was waiting for us. When we opened the doors, everyone was in the back. I hopped in happy as hell.

"What the fuck yo' ass sitting up here looking like a fucking glow worm for?"

"Don't fucking start, Shamaad, I just got in the limo."

"I just asked yo' light bright ass a question," Shamaad rolled his eyes long and hard.

"Anyway," I laughed and returned the favor. "I'm getting married."

I flashed my ring in the center aisle.

"O. M. Geeeeeeeee!" Reign squealed. "About time! I thought I was gon' die keeping that a secret."

"Wait bitch, you knew?"

"Duh," she looked around and the other girls were looking everywhere but at me. "We all knew. He just never told us when he was planning to do it and he told me to stop asking and mind my got damn business," Reign tilted her head at Christian and he laughed.

"Well, shit, you were getting on my got damn nerves," he said and then ducked to get away from her pocketbook that she had just thrown.

"Ivy surprised me tonight, too."

"Whoooooooo, thank goodness, 'cause that was a hard secret to keep too," Jess said and then looked away because she didn't mean to just tell on herself.

"Oh, so you knew I was doing to be a daddy before I did?"

"Who the hell did you think took her crybaby ass to the doctor?" Reign asked.

"Whatever. Tonight is just full of surprises and I can't wait to chill and celebrate."

"Turn up," Reign toasted her ginger ale.

About 30 minutes later, we were pulling up and when I say people came to show love, they did just that. The line was around the building and the setup was so nice. The black carpet was amazing and we had hired so many photographers to capture the moments of tonight. There were newscasters, and everyone who was everyone was in attendance. Tonight was about us and I couldn't be any happier than I was in this moment.

I looked over at Christian and mouthed the words I love you, and he reciprocated.

For once, everything was coming together and it looked like Ivy Richards, soon to be Hope, was getting her happily ever after, after all. Sometimes you had to play a fool for love and that didn't make you weak, it made you human. Sometimes, we had to take things for what they are. I wasn't saying in no way shape or form to sit and let a man run over you, but sometimes it was worth it to forgive. But like I said before, "Fool me once shame on you, Fool me twice...."

You know how it goes.

THE END!